Reid felt as good as he looked, all soft lips and solid body. And he tasted good too. Whiskey. Chocolate. Heaven. Jaxon's appetite returned in full force, but it wasn't airplane steak he was ravenous for.

Jaxon let go of the tie, but only so he could grasp Reid's shoulders instead, and Reid responded in kind. For a glorious few seconds, they made out like horny teenagers.

But before Jaxon could work out the logistics of joining the mile-high club—well, *rejoining*, since he was already a repeat member—Reid pulled away. He got off the bed and stood in the narrow space next to it, adjusting his tie. "We can't do that," he said evenly.

"Don't tell me you're not into guys, 'cause you were pretty into it." For a moment anyway.

Reid shook his head. "This is a critical mission, and I'm your assistant. I need to make sure everything goes smoothly."

WELCOME TO

DREAMSPUN DESIRES

Dear Reader,

Love is the dream. It dazzles us, makes us stronger, and brings us to our knees. Dreamspun Desires tell stories of love featuring your favorite heartwarming heroes, captivating plots, and exotic locations. Stories that make your breath catch and your imagination soar.

In the pages of these wonderful love stories, readers can escape to a world where love conquers all, the tenderness of a first kiss sweeps you away, and your heart pounds at the sight of the one you love.

When you put it all together, you find romance in its truest form.

Love always finds a way.

Elizabeth North

Executive Director
Dreamspinner Press

Kim Fielding

THE SPY'S LOVE SONG

DREAMSPUN DESIRES

PUBLISHED BY

DREAMSPINNER
PRESS

Published by
DREAMSPINNER PRESS

5032 Capital Circle SW, Suite 2, PMB# 279,
Tallahassee, FL 32305-7886 USA
www.dreamspinnerpress.com

This is a work of fiction. Names, characters, places, and incidents either
are the product of author imagination or are used fictitiously, and any
resemblance to actual persons, living or dead, business establishments,
events, or locales is entirely coincidental.

Paperback ISBN: 978-1-64108-055-2
Digital ISBN: 978-1-64080-502-6
Library of Congress Control Number: 2017919628
Paperback published October 2018
v. 1.0

Printed in the United States of America
∞
This paper meets the requirements of
ANSI/NISO Z39.48-1992 (Permanence of Paper).

KIM FIELDING is very pleased every time someone calls her eclectic. Her books have won Rainbow Awards and span a variety of genres. She has migrated back and forth across the western two-thirds of the United States and currently lives in California, where she long ago ran out of bookshelf space. She's a university professor who dreams of being able to travel and write full-time. She also dreams of having two perfectly behaved children, a husband who isn't obsessed with football, and a house that cleans itself. Some dreams are more easily obtained than others.

Blogs: kfieldingwrites.com and www.goodreads.com/author/show/4105707.Kim_Fielding/blog

Facebook: www.facebook.com/KFieldingWrites

Email: kim@kfieldingwrites.com

Twitter: @KFieldingWrites

By Kim Fielding

DREAMSPUN BEYOND
#8 – Ante Up

DREAMSPUN DESIRES
#56 – A Full Plate
#67 – The Spy's Love Song

Published by **DREAMSPINNER PRESS**
www.dreamspinnerpress.com

Chapter One

A NAKED young man lay faceup on the billiard table, snoring softly. Lipstick smeared his face, but Jaxson couldn't tell whether it was the kid's own or if it had transferred from someone else's mouth. The kid looked more comfortable than the other young man—this one wearing a leopard-print jock—who was curled on the hard tile under the billiard table, twitching in his sleep.

If Jaxon had learned their names, he didn't remember them. Just as he couldn't recall the names of the people scattered in the living room and bedrooms or the pretty woman in the armchair in the library. He didn't care what any of them were called. At the moment, the only thing he wanted to know was where to find a goddamn bathroom. There had to be several of them in this overblown suite, right? But all he managed was a bleary circuit through toiletless rooms.

He'd almost decided to piss into a large potted ficus when a dapper gentleman in a well-tailored suit appeared. "May I help you, Mr. Powers?" His tone suggested he was accustomed to dealing with people whose brains weren't fully functional.

"Bathroom?"

"Right this way."

The man's name was Roger Diggs. Jaxon remembered that. He was a butler who came with the suite. As Diggs led the way through the kitchen—its gleaming surfaces cluttered with empty bottles and takeout containers—Jaxon wondered what it would be like to have a career as a hotel amenity. Maybe not so bad. Diggs looked cheerful enough, not even batting an eye at the threesome snoozing on the floor in front of the dual fridges.

Jaxon had the enormous bathroom to himself. He felt better after emptying his bladder and splashing cold water on his face, although he carefully avoided glancing in the mirrors. Whenever he was sober, fully rested, and took time to shave and deal with his curly hair, he looked pretty good for a guy who'd recently stared down thirty-seven. This morning, though—if it was still morning—he probably resembled an extra in a zombie flick.

Diggs waited patiently just outside the bathroom. "Your phone's been ringing, Mr. Powers. Frequently."

"Ringing or playing a song?"

"A song." The corner of Diggs's mouth twitched. "The Notorious B.I.G., I believe."

Shit. Jaxon rubbed his face. "Can you, um, point me to—"

"I have your phone right here. I hope you don't mind that I took the liberty." Diggs removed it from his inside suit pocket and handed it over.

Just as Jaxon took the phone, it began to belt out "Mo Money Mo Problems," a tune almost as familiar to him as his own songs. Instead of answering, Jaxon glared at the screen until the music stopped.

"Perhaps," Diggs began smoothly, "you'd like to take your call out on the terrace? It's an unusually warm day. I can bring you coffee and a light breakfast."

Jaxon's stomach lurched. "Okay. Yes on the coffee, but I'll skip the food."

"Not even some toast?"

After consulting with his innards, Jaxon gave a cautious nod. "Dry."

"Excellent. Follow me, please."

They walked back through the kitchen, into the library, and up a set of stairs leading to a second floor of books. Then, to Jaxon's surprise, Diggs tugged on one of the shelves. The hidden door led to a wide terrace that looked as if it had been transplanted from a Mediterranean palace. A tiled fountain burbled cheerfully in front of a panorama of the San Francisco skyline. Jaxon squinted at the sky. "Sun's out."

"If it's too bright, I can—"

"It's fine." Maybe the light would help clear his head. He collapsed onto one of the patio chairs. "That coffee would be great now."

"Right away. And your guests?" Diggs didn't even pause before he said *guests*. The guy deserved a medal.

"Clear 'em out, please. I'll pay for their Ubers or whatever. Just…." Jaxon waved vaguely.

"Of course."

Jaxon was left alone with his phone and the view of the Transamerica Pyramid. Diggs had been right about the weather. Although Jaxon wore nothing but last night's jeans and T-shirt, the temperature was comfortable—a rarity for early June in San Francisco, but pleasant. It had been years since he spent many daytime hours outside, and his skin eagerly soaked up the warmth. Maybe he was suffering from a vitamin D deficiency.

Although the phone played again, Jaxon set it on the table and waited. The chair wasn't as comfy as he'd hoped. For twenty grand a night, you'd think the hotel could manage outdoor furniture with padded armrests. Jaxon considered asking Diggs to find him something better, but then rejected the idea. Diggs probably had his hands full already.

As if on cue, the butler appeared with an oversize china mug and matching plate, which he set on the table near Jaxon. "No cream or sugar, correct?"

"Yeah. Thanks." The coffee smelled wonderful, like a magic potion guaranteed to cure what ailed him, and the plate contained four triangles of wheat toast with a garnish of yellow and orange flower petals.

"Your guests have left. May I get you anything else?"

"No. Thanks."

"All right. Just text if you need anything." Diggs bobbed his head before going inside.

Jaxon managed to eat half of the toast, and although the coffee wasn't a magical cure, it did help him feel more human. Just as he was deciding whether to text Diggs and ask for a refill, the damn phone began to sing again. This time Jaxon answered.

"Hi, Buzz."

"Top o' the mornin', Sleeping Beauty." As always, he sounded unreasonably cheery, as if life was one big celebration, complete with balloons and confetti. Buzz Baker was the man who managed Jaxon Powers's career. And to a large extent, managed Jaxon's life as well. Which was why Jaxon was currently in San Francisco while Buzz was in LA—Jaxon was tired of being managed.

"What." Jaxon knew he sounded petulant but couldn't help it.

"How do you like the hotel?"

"I don't know. It's okay. I think I want to go somewhere else, though. Somewhere quiet." He wasn't sure where. It seemed as though no matter where he went—the desert, the countryside, tiny tropical islands, mountaintop lodges—he ended up with a retinue. He'd wake up in the mornings to find pretty strangers drooling on the billiard tables or grinning at him from the hot tub. He used to find them in his bed too, although that happened less often since he'd become better at saying *no thanks*.

"Sure, sure. Give me a few hours and I'll come up with something. How do you feel about shipboard living?"

Jaxon sighed. "I don't know."

"I'll see what I can do. But that's not why I called. For tonight, I need you to stay put and get some sleep. We have a 9:00 a.m. meeting at your hotel."

"Meeting? Why?"

"To talk about a super-exciting gig."

Jaxon tipped his head back and groaned. "No. I don't even want to *think* about another tour right now. I'm nowhere close to recording the next album, and—"

"Not a tour, babe. Just one gig—but it's a doozy. Special."

"Are you gonna let me in on the details?"

"Sure thing, cupcake. Tomorrow at nine. For now I want you to get some rest, maybe do some work. Take a walk around Frisco!"

"Nobody really calls it that, Buzz." Nobody except tourists from Indiana.

Buzz just laughed. "Eat clam chowder in a sourdough bowl. Ride a cable car. Buy souvenir back scratchers and paper lanterns in Chinatown. Pretend you're not a jaded son of a bitch."

When Buzz refused to talk about anything else except where to eat in San Francisco, Jaxon ended the call. He found his way to a shower—encountering nobody along the way except Diggs and some of the housekeeping staff—and later to the bedroom that housed his clothes. He needed to tell Buzz to stop booking such ridiculously large suites.

Dressed and more or less sentient, Jaxon took Buzz's advice and went for a walk. He didn't have the energy for a run. It was a glorious day in a beautiful city, with the bay sparkling like a jewel and a light breeze relaying the clang of a cable car. But despite the knit cap covering Jaxon's famous red curls, people recognized him. And because San Francisco wasn't as used to celebrities as were LA and New York, people stared and pointed. They took photos with their phones. And quite a few of them stopped him to ask for autographs or selfies.

He tried to be gracious with his fans; he really did. For one thing, he could still remember the rush of excitement when he was a teen and he met his idols in person. For another, if it weren't for these fans, he wouldn't be able to afford the obscenely expensive hotel suites. He'd still be stuck in a tiny town in the Nebraska Sandhills, maybe selling insurance to farmers and ranchers, as his dad did, or cutting and styling hair alongside his mom. He was grateful to his fans—but they made enjoying a simple stroll almost impossible.

After only a few blocks, Jaxon gave up and returned to the hotel. He considered going for a drive—up into Marin, perhaps, or down to Big Sur—but decided he didn't want to be cooped up inside a car with only his own company.

Diggs met him inside the suite. "May I get you anything, sir?"

"No. Well, yes. Do you know a place to get good pizza?"

"Of course, several." Diggs smiled. "My favorite is in North Beach."

"Could you get a pie brought to me around seven tonight? Nothing fancy—just pepperoni. And some decent beer to go with it?"

"Naturally."

"Thanks."

A grand piano dominated a portion of the living room. Jaxon sat on the bench and began to play. He wasn't an especially good pianist—his best instruments were guitars and his voice—but it seemed a shame to ignore the piano when it was sitting there, waiting. He ran through a few of his own songs, humming along but not singing, and then experimented with some new tunes. He'd already composed several for the next album, but he needed a few more, and he was having trouble coming up with anything satisfactory. Everything felt like a rehash of the stuff he'd been doing a decade earlier. Maybe he needed a new muse.

He played for hours without getting anywhere. Then Diggs brought him two six-packs of mixed microbrews and that pizza—as delicious as promised—and Jaxon ate alone at a dining table that could have seated twenty. Although he drank enough to get seriously buzzed, he didn't go out to a club, didn't make any effort to gather strangers eager to party with a rock star. Instead he soaked in a huge tub and watched *Vertigo*, sipping enough beer to keep from getting sober. It was still early when he chose a bedroom at random, fell onto the mattress, and sank into sleep.

Chapter Two

"OATMEAL." Jaxon lifted the spoon and let the contents glop back into the bowl.

"It's very good oatmeal," Diggs said. "But I can get you something else if you'd prefer."

Jaxon had awakened at the unholy hour of 8:00 a.m. and had taken a quick shower before settling on the terrace with coffee and breakfast. One of San Francisco's signature fogs shrouded the city, so he wore a hoodie and his wool hat. Despite the chill, the eerie view was nice. He wasn't so sure about breakfast, though.

"Do you live here at the hotel?" he asked.

Diggs chuckled. "No, I have an apartment in Oakland. But the hotel sometimes provides temporary quarters when I'm engaged with special clients."

"You mean when you're stuck with pains in the ass like me."

"You're not a pain at all."

"I saw what this place looked like yesterday morning, dude. It was a mess."

Diggs shrugged. "Easily cleaned. Believe me, I've worked with many guests who were difficult. You're not one of them."

"I guess I'll have to step up my game," Jaxon joked. "Wouldn't want to wreck my reputation."

"If you like, I'll tell everyone you exhausted me with your constant demands and wild ways," Diggs said.

Once upon a time, Jaxon would have exhausted him in exactly that manner. He would have awakened next to the naked man on the billiard table—equally naked himself—and instead of clearing out the guests, he'd have resumed the party with more booze, more food, more drugs, more sex. Then, in a few days, he'd have moved on to the next hotel in the next city, leaving Buzz to pay for the damage he'd left behind. But here he was now—up before nine, wearing clean clothes, and eating oatmeal.

"Do you have family?" Jaxon asked. Then he winced. "Sorry. That's none of my business."

"I don't mind. I divorced years ago, but I have a son at Stanford. Biomedical computation. He's doing very well."

"Wow, that's great. Congratulations. But you never remarried?" As if to make up for the prying questions, Jaxon swallowed some oatmeal. It wasn't bad, actually.

Unflappable as always, Diggs smiled and shook his head. "I'm married to my job. It's a happy union."

"Really? Dealing with spoiled rich assholes doesn't get to you?"

"I've met some of the world's most fascinating people, and I've made their complicated lives a bit smoother. I find that rewarding."

Before Jaxon could ask another question, his phone dinged, and he glanced at the screen. It was Buzz. *Be ready in 15.*

Jaxon started to type a smartass reply, erased it, and simply sent a thumbs-up. He was pissed at Buzz for being secretive about this meeting, yet he knew he deserved it. He hadn't exactly been an easy client. And sure, Buzz made a lot of money off him, but Buzz worked damn hard for it.

Fifteen minutes later, Diggs let him know that Jaxon's guests had arrived in the hotel lobby. "Coffee for everyone?" he asked.

"Yeah, I guess. Um, in the library." If he was going to act like a grown-up, that room seemed like the most adult place to have a meeting.

"Of course."

The library was circular, and Jaxon was pacing its edge when he heard Buzz's familiar voice. A moment later Buzz entered the room accompanied by a woman and two men in sober suits. Buzz wore a suit too, but his was crimson, with a canary silk shirt and matching yellow shoes. He performed quick introductions. The woman, thin and fiftyish, was Diana Chiu, and her body language suggested she was in charge. Clark Durant was a mousy-looking man, the type who seemed as if he'd been born with a calculator in his hand. And Reid Stanfill took Jaxon's breath away. He was tall, rock solid, and square-jawed, with buzz-cut dark hair and amber eyes that laser-focused on Jaxon. Chiu and Durant smiled as they shook Jaxon's hand, but Stanfill did not. And he didn't try to prove his manliness by squeezing Jaxon's hand to a pulp, maybe because he knew Jaxon needed that hand to play guitar.

Diggs wheeled in a cart bearing a sterling silver coffeepot and creamer, bone china cups and saucers, and a dizzying array of sweeteners. "Just text if you need anything, sir," he said to Jaxon before gracefully retreating.

Stanfill snorted quietly—and didn't look remotely ashamed when Jaxon shot him a glare.

Buzz led a round of small talk as he poured. Jaxon wasn't at all surprised that Stanfill took his coffee black and without sugar. When the rest of them took their seats, Stanfill stood near the library doors like a sentinel, his huge paw dwarfing the china cup. Jaxon sat behind the large desk, which made him feel like a captain of industry instead of some guy who sang and played guitar.

"So," he said loudly, interrupting a discussion of the weather, "what's the gig?" If there *was* a gig. None of these people looked like promoters. To his surprise, Stanfill almost cracked a smile. He apparently approved of a direct approach. Bully for him.

It was Chiu who answered. "Mr. Powers, we're—"

"Jaxon."

She nodded. "Jaxon, then. I work for the State Department. I have the opportunity to invite you—"

Jaxon set his cup down hard enough to splash coffee onto the desk. "Nope. No way am I going to let anyone trot me out to perform for the president like a trained monkey." He crossed his arms for good measure.

"That's not what we're asking. The State Department has responsibility over foreign affairs." She might have been trying to avoid condescension, but she didn't quite manage it.

"Oh," said Jaxon. Maybe he should have known that, but he'd spent most of his high school government class either stoned or composing songs in his head. Actually, that was how he'd spent pretty much *all* of his high school classes. "Sorry. Go ahead."

She leaned forward in her seat. "Do you know much about Vasnytsia?"

"Um, it's a country, right? Somewhere in the middle of all the -stan countries maybe?"

"A little west of there, but you're close. It's in Eastern Europe."

"Okay." Jaxon had performed many European concerts, but not there. At least he didn't think so. On some of the tours, the countries had blended together, especially back when he spent a good chunk of his offstage time partying.

She turned to her smaller colleague. "Clark, could you give him a briefing?"

Clark must have been one of those grade-school kids who loved getting called on. Now he lifted his shoulders and straightened his tie. "During the time of the Soviet Union, Vasnytsia operated as an independent country. It wasn't part of the USSR, but it was communist. It had a population of less than four million and, completely landlocked, its economy relied primarily on agriculture and some industry. It was run by a dictator who did an excellent job of playing off both the West and Moscow. He got arms and goods from both sides. Then the Iron Curtain fell, and—"

"Is there going to be a test?" Jaxon interrupted. "Should I be taking notes? Ooh! Can I earn extra credit?" Then he felt bad for his outburst because Durant looked so disappointed. Chiu remained expressionless—she was probably a great poker player—and Buzz rolled his eyes. Stanfill, though, lowered his brows and allowed his lip to curl slightly.

"May I continue?" Durant asked after a short pause.

"Yeah. Sorry. Go ahead."

More tie straightening. "After the Iron Curtain fell, Vasnytsia's ruler was worried that a similar democratic revolution would reach his country. He built up the military police and sealed off the borders, all while strictly controlling citizens' access to the media. And he cracked down on dissent. We… can't divulge the details"—he glanced at Chiu as if for permission—"but I can tell you that anyone who spoke out against the regime was dealt with harshly."

Jaxon pushed his cup away. "That sounds lovely."

"The dictator died a few years ago and was succeeded by his son, a man named Bogdan Talmirov. He styles himself a prime minister and claims to hold elections, but last time he won 98 percent of the vote."

"Sounds like a popular guy."

"Unlikely," Durant said. "He continues to forbid access to the internet and to anything but state-run or state-approved media. He almost never allows citizens to leave, and very few foreigners are allowed in. The ones he does let in are shadowed constantly by government-supplied guides. He's still punitive against any opposition. And he's probably still stockpiling weapons, only now it's Russia he's playing off against the West."

Durant stopped speaking, as if he were waiting for Jaxon's questions. Jaxon looked at Stanfill and was gratified to discover the big man looked as impatient as Jaxon felt. God, the man was hot. He probably spent a lot of time in the gym. And despite his broad shoulders and slim waist, his suit fit perfectly. Custom tailored.

Not designer threads like Jaxon wore, and certainly not flashy like Buzz's outfits, but good quality. Too bad he was wearing a suit jacket, because those trousers probably caressed a solid ass like—

"Jaxon?" That was Chiu, her tone crisp.

"Look, I appreciate the lesson in history or geography or whatever, but what does any of this have to do with me?"

She smiled. "It turns out that Prime Minister Talmirov is a fan of yours."

"I thought outside stuff wasn't allowed in his country."

"Not for ordinary people. Talmirov can access whatever he likes."

"Of course he can. Fine. I'll send him an autograph." Although Jaxon was being flippant, he was somewhat disturbed to learn a tyrant loved his music. Not that Jaxon had any control over that. Hell, he had millions of fans; some of them were undoubtedly scumbags. Jaxon's songs didn't encourage scumbaggery, though. They were almost all about the usual things—love and sex. Mostly sex.

Chiu set her empty cup and saucer on the little table nearby. "Talmirov has requested you to perform two special concerts in the capital, Starograd. It's a unique opportunity—the first time he's invited anyone from outside the country."

"Right." Jaxon tipped his head back to stare at the library's domed ceiling, which featured a mural of constellations. That was a pretty cool idea. Next time he bought a place, he'd have a ceiling mural put in the bedroom. Maybe with little twinkly lights for the stars. After a moment, he turned back to Chiu. "You're gonna have to send my regrets. I'm not touring right now."

"The compensation will be substantial."

"Do I *look* like I need more money? Go talk to your pals at the IRS. They'll tell you my income is comfy as is."

For the first time, her composure slipped. Only for a moment, though. "Then do it for your country. You have the opportunity to make a real contribution."

"By singing a couple of songs?"

Apparently it was time for Durant—Mr. Exposition himself—to chime in. "Our relationship with Vasnytsia is strained at best. And that's problematic, because while the country is small, it enjoys a strategic location. If they turn away from us entirely, they'll give Russia a better chance to, well, disrupt things. As in Crimea. But if we can strengthen our ties with Vasnytsia, our position vis-à-vis Russia will be improved."

The guy used *vis-à-vis* in a sentence. Wow.

Jaxon tried to formulate a way to refuse without sounding like an asswipe. But then Stanfill took a step nearer and spoke for the first time since they'd been introduced. "Four million people live in Vasnytsia. If this goes well, you'll be helping to improve their lives."

"And making the world safer for Truth, Justice, and the American Way?"

Stanfill didn't crack a smile. "Something like that."

"Just by singing a few tunes? C'mon. Even I'm not bigheaded enough to think my music's *that* special."

"It's not the music itself. It's you acting as our country's representative. If we reach out to Talmirov like this—if *you* reach out—he may come to see us all in a better light. He might turn to us more than he does to Moscow."

"That sounds pretty lame."

Stanfill shrugged his broad shoulders. "It's a small step. Sometimes big changes have to start small."

Jaxon's chair scraped on the tile as he pushed back. He turned away from his visitors and faced a library shelf, running his fingers over the spines of the books. The volumes varied in topic and looked as if they were well read. He wondered who chose them. Diggs maybe? Or did a hotel functionary just scoop them up at random from used-book stores and library sales?

Nobody interrupted him. Maybe he should have felt powerful, making all these people wait. But all he felt was exhausted. He suddenly yearned for a tiny cabin with a big bed and no cell service. He'd sit on the balcony and play acoustic music for the birds and the deer.

"I'll do it," he said quietly.

When he turned around and saw the relief on Stanfill's face, he was at least a little glad for his decision.

A flurry of conversation followed between Buzz, Chiu, and Durant. Stanfill remained silent, staring at Jaxon, and Jaxon stared back. He didn't pay attention to what anyone was saying; Buzz could fill him in on the important details later. He thought instead what it would be like to peel off Stanfill's clothing, to feel those big hands running over his skin. Would that short haircut feel soft or bristly? Would Stanfill smell like cologne?

Jaxon had the impression Stanfill knew exactly what was running through his head. But the handsome face remained expressionless, and the heat in those eyes could have been from annoyance or anger.

Finally Jaxon had enough. "Look," he said, interrupting Buzz in midspeech, "you can work it out without me. You know what I like. Cabrera and his band did a good job backing me up last time I was on tour, so see if they're available. And I don't need a whole entourage if it's only gonna be two shows, so—"

"You don't understand," Chiu interrupted.

"What don't I understand?"

Buzz patted Jaxon's shoulder. "This prime minister dude, he's not letting anyone into his country except you and one assistant. His people will provide your support on their end. But don't worry, kiddo. It's only for a few days. You'll be in and out, everything smooth as butter."

"Or lube," Jaxon muttered. "Fine. As long as I don't have to share a bedroom with you. You snore."

"I'm not going, Jax. You need someone who speaks the local lingo, and that ain't me."

"But who…?"

Perfectly on cue, Stanfill stepped forward. "Me."

Shit.

Chapter Three

BUZZ sent a courier with books about Vasnytsia, but Jaxon left them in the suite's library, along with an envelope bearing Diggs's name. The enclosed check would go a good way toward defraying college expenses for the younger Diggs. Jaxon packed up his guitar and some clothing and flew to a tech billionaire's private estate in Hawaii, where he spent a week sitting on the sand and rolling in bed with an A-list actor. Jaxon and Chris had been having occasional flings for years, but they'd agreed they would never be anything but fuck buddies. Chris was deep in the closet and intended to stay there as long as he kept bringing in action-hero roles. Once upon a time, Jaxon hadn't cared. Chris was fun, nothing more. Most recently, though, Jaxon left Hawaii unsatisfied, as if his days there had eaten away a bit of him.

He spent the following weeks in a fairly modest New York City apartment on the Upper East Side. He didn't let Buzz hire any staff to take care of him, mostly because he wanted solitude amid the sea of humanity. He had most of his meals delivered and watched a lot of old movies, and for some reason, he found himself playing a lot of ancient Johnny Cash tunes. He went to a few parties, but other than that, he remained sober. It was nice to know he could.

He flew to Washington, DC, and climbed onto a large private jet. Stanfill was already on board, waiting for him. Apparently they were the only passengers.

"I hope my tax dollars aren't paying for this," said Jaxon as he belted himself into one of the plush seats.

Stanfill didn't look up from his phone. "Vasnytsian tax dollars."

A smiling young woman brought drinks—Scotch for Jaxon and ice water for Stanfill—and explained some of the airplane's features. Then she gave them the required safety spiel before disappearing gracefully into the cockpit.

Stanfill remained silent and intent on his phone as the plane taxied and took off. Jaxon could have entertained himself with his own phone or with the movies and Wi-Fi available on the cabin's big screen. But he found it more interesting to stare at Stanfill, who wore another nicely tailored suit. His hair looked freshly trimmed, his cheeks were free of stubble, and although his suit jacket likely hung in the plane's cleverly disguised closet, he hadn't taken off his tie.

"Who do you work for?" Jaxon asked loudly.

"Government."

"Yeah, but what part of the government? What's your actual job?"

Stanfill scowled. "I'm your assistant." Okay, that meant Jaxon could start thinking of him as Reid.

"Since you're my assistant, you can get me a refill." Jaxon waggled his empty glass. "And some peanuts."

"You can get your own. Or call the flight attendant."

"But you're my assistant. You're supposed to assist me."

After a moment of silent glaring, Reid unbuckled and stood. He grabbed Jaxon's glass and stomped over to the drinks cabinet. He poured a healthy shot of whiskey into the glass and then stomped back. But when Jaxon reached for the glass, Reid emptied it in one long swallow, slammed it down on the table beside Jaxon, and collapsed into his own seat with a smirk.

"Just how is that assisting me?" Jaxon demanded.

"If I have a few drinks, I'm less likely to strangle you. I think that's very helpful."

Maybe Reid thought he was winning some kind of battle, but it had been a long time since anyone but Buzz had given Jaxon grief. This could be way more fun than being stuck with a kiss-ass. Jaxon smiled. "You drank from my glass. How do you know you won't catch my nasty cooties?"

"Alcohol kills cooties."

"What if I have superstrength cooties? Alcohol-resistant ones?"

"Your cooties don't scare me."

Reid's eyes definitely held a challenge, but Jaxon was uncertain about the nature of the contest. Was Reid attracted to him?

"You know I'm a depraved rock star, right?"

Reid answered with a snort.

"And not only that. I'm queer as a three-dollar bill. Well, I've slept with ladies now and then over the years, but I prefer men."

"I've been briefed on your background."

"Briefed." It was Jaxon's turn to snort. "And you don't care?"

"Look." Reid leaned forward slightly, narrowing the distance between them. "My job is to get you through this trip without incident. I don't care who you've slept with. All I care about is that you show up, you sing your songs, and you get the hell out of Vasnytsia without causing an international crisis. You manage that and you can spend the rest of your life shacking up with a herd of sheep and the Mormon Tabernacle Choir, and I won't lose any sleep over it." He leaned back and picked up his phone again.

They remained silent for a few hundred miles, and then Jaxon got his own refill and grabbed some packets of peanuts. When he returned to his seat, he tossed one of them in Reid's general direction. Reid caught it neatly in midair, seemingly without moving his gaze from his screen.

A few minutes later, Jaxon shifted in his seat. "Where are you from, Reid?"

"I'm stationed in DC right now."

"Okay, but are you from there originally?"

Reid set his phone aside. "Grew up in Ohio. Spent four years in the Army. Went to college in California, got a degree in Slavic languages, signed on with the government."

"Wow. I bet you could fit that entire biography in one tweet. It's a good thing you're not originally from Mississippi, though. That would put you over 140 characters."

"I don't tweet," Reid said, as if it were something obscene.

"Of course not. You don't strike me as the social-media type. Antisocial media more like." Jaxon went full steam ahead. "What about family? Wife? Two-point-three kids? A German shepherd at least?"

"Parents are dead. I'm single. No pets."

Jaxon wasn't certain whether that last bit was an attempt at humor. It was hard to read Reid. He kept his tone flat and his face nearly expressionless most of the time, but those eyes… he couldn't control whatever was sparking in those eyes. Trouble was, without any other cues, Jaxon couldn't identify the emotion, which both frustrated and fascinated him. Usually Jaxon knew exactly what people wanted from him—money, sex, endorsements, or just the simple validation of having a celebrity pay them attention. But Jaxon had no idea what Reid wanted. Aside from a lack of international incidents.

"Okay. So nothing you just told me about yourself gives me any confidence that you know how to plan a concert. I guess you can talk to the locals, but even a small gig gets complicated. There's the setup, the equipment, the crowd control…. Plus I have only a few days to practice with a band I've never met before."

Reid surprised him with a wide, genuine smile. Of course he was even more handsome when he grinned, dammit. "*Those* were good points. Considerably more relevant than anything else you've brought up."

"Well, you might think I'm just a grown-up kid who plays for a living, but I'm a professional. It's important that my performances go well. Important to me—not just to the future of democracy in Europe."

Reid nodded. And this time when he went to the drinks cabinet, he brought refills for them both. And pretzels. "I've had experience in logistics," he said as he sat down. "First in the Army, then in my current job. Not concerts, but I've planned a lot of complex operations that included large numbers of personnel and a variety of equipment. Plus I've spent the last weeks interviewing your manager and several other music managers, agents, and promoters. I'm good." He sounded supremely confident.

"Fine. I don't want to suck, okay?"

"I'll do my best to ensure the success of the mission."

Not long after that, the flight attendant brought dinner. It was a decent enough meal—steak, pasta, and greens—but Jaxon only picked at his. After Reid cleaned his own plate and polished off a slice of chocolate raspberry cake, he pointed his fork at Jaxon. "I hope you're not counting on kale, quinoa, and tofu in Starograd, because you're not likely to find them. Food in Vasnytsia is basic Eastern European."

"Cabbage and dumplings?"

"Something like that."

Jaxon pushed his plate away. "I'm just not very hungry right now." Even after all these years, flying unsettled his stomach. "I'm not a picky eater."

Reid raised his eyebrows skeptically.

"Really," Jaxon insisted. "I grew up in Peril, Nebraska. Population two thousand. We ate beef from my uncle's ranch and vegetables from cans. I'm pretty sure the only spices in the cupboard were salt and pepper. I never even saw a bagel until I left home at seventeen. And then for a few years, I was dirt poor. I ate whatever I could get my hands on." More than once, he'd scrounged trash bins outside grocery stores and restaurants. He wasn't proud of that history, but he wasn't ashamed either. He'd done what he needed to survive, and he hadn't hurt anyone along the way. That was good enough.

"You're not starving now," Reid pointed out.

"Not for years. But I remember what it was like."

Reid set down the fork and drained his glass of water. Like Jaxon, he'd given up on the booze. "That hotel suite you had in San Francisco? With what you paid for a single night, a dozen families in India could live comfortably for a year."

Jaxon set his jaw. "I've done benefit concerts. I donate to a lot of charities."

"Right."

Having had enough of this conversation, Jaxon stood abruptly, nearly bumping into the flight attendant, who'd come to collect their dishes. "Coffee?" she asked.

He shook his head.

Two beds had been set up near the back of the plane. Actual real beds, not the torture chambers commercial airlines expected you to sleep on. The farther one was separated from the main cabin by a partial wall. Jaxon had found that the best way to deal with the eastbound time change was to remain awake on overnight flights. Then he'd be good and ready to snooze when it was bedtime in Europe. Since he had no plans to sleep now, he took his acoustic guitar out of the closet where the attendant had stowed it, kicked off his shoes, and sat on the rearmost bed.

When he got in a mood like this, he didn't consciously choose what to play; his fingers made the decision for him. He often wasn't even aware what the song was. The music seemed to flow, perhaps directed by some muse who temporarily possessed his body. His mind sailed along with the notes, as insentient as a leaf floating on a stream. When Jaxon played like this, it was for himself alone. A meditation, a prayer.

So it was with a start that he realized Reid was leaning in the doorway, watching him. Jaxon had no idea how long he'd been there. He stopped playing, and for a long moment they stared at each other.

"Sorry. Am I keeping you awake?" He noted that Reid was still fully dressed.

"That's not your usual style," Reid said quietly.

Jaxon had to think about what he'd been playing. "It's an old Janis Ian tune." Definitely *not* his usual style, which he usually described as postpunk alternative rock with a strong lean toward pop. That sounded impressive and official. He'd read articles in which genre pundits argued over which category his work belonged in. As Buzz liked to remind him, it didn't matter what anybody called it as long as they paid to listen to it.

"It's sad," Reid said, referring to the song. "Or no. Wistful?"

A rush of warmth flooded Jaxon. Instead of demanding Jaxon play one of his big hits, Reid was attempting to understand him. Reid was going for communication, not entertainment. Hardly anyone did that with Jaxon.

"My grandma used to listen to folk music and country-western. When I was a little kid, I'd go to her house after school—she lived just a few doors down—and she'd put on her records. Scratchy old things. I used to tease her about them, but really, I loved them. We'd sing together." Jaxon smiled at a memory he hadn't relived in ages. "She had a good voice."

"Is she still alive?"

"No. She died of lung cancer during my junior year of high school. She never got to see me become famous."

Reid didn't offer any tired condolences, but his small nod suggested he knew what that type of loss felt like. He'd said his parents were dead, hadn't he? He ran his palm across the top of his hair. "Do you ever go back to Peril?"

"Nope. My parents and I didn't part on the best terms." Understatement. They expected college, heterosexuality, and eventual marriage; he wanted a music career and varied sleeping partners. There had been a lot of yelling. The day after he graduated high school, he'd packed up some clothes, his guitar, and all the money he possessed, and he'd hitched a ride to Ogallala, where he got on a Greyhound heading west. Stupid-ass move, but it had saved his life. Peril would have smothered him.

"Maybe you should return sometime," said Reid.

"Maybe."

Another long silence contained a whole lot of unspoken words. Then Reid twitched a shoulder. "Didn't mean to interrupt." He turned as if to go.

"Reid?"

"Yeah?" Pausing, Reid looked back over his shoulder.

"You can stay if you want. I don't mind an audience."

That mystery emotion flared in Reid's eyes again. Then he nodded and removed his shoes, carefully lining them up near the wall. With a small grin, he stretched out on the bed beside Jaxon, propping his back against the padded headboard. For the first time since they'd met, Reid looked almost relaxed. Except for the damned tie.

"When did you change the spelling of your name?" Reid asked.

Jaxon blinked. "You know about that?"

"I told you. I was briefed on your background. Plus any idiot could deduce that in 1981, no parents in Peril, Nebraska, were going to name their kid Jaxon-with-an-x."

To his surprise, Jaxon laughed. "You got me there. I switched the *cks* to *x* as soon as I left. I thought it looked cooler that way. I had it legally changed after I got my first gold record. Were you always Reid?"

Reid's expression had been almost open—for Reid—but now it closed up again. "Yes."

All right. Apparently Jaxon's history was an open book while Reid's past was a no-man's-land. Jaxon began to strum again, idly picking out chords until a tune coalesced. Ah. Roy Orbison. Jaxon's subconscious was in an oldies mood. He crooned along, keeping his voice just loud enough to carry over the engine noise, feeling the familiar thrill as his throat magically roller-coastered through the highs and lows. Reid watched him closely, his body only inches away. After Roy Orbison, Jaxon followed a natural segue into Carl Perkins and then a slide into Elvis, and then he found himself in the blues, channeling a bit of Bessie Smith and Muddy Waters. It was all very fine. But after that he somehow found himself purring a torch song—in French, no less.

When he finished, his hands fell still and he set the guitar aside.

"'*Ne me quitte pas*'? Don't leave me?" asked Reid after a moment.

"Jacques Brel. Another of Gram's favorites."

Reid's eyes were like lasers. "Who left you?"

"Nobody. I just— Oh. You speak French too, huh?"

"It's not my best language, but I can manage." Reid wasn't fooled by Jaxon's attempt to sidestep the question. Jaxon could almost see the gears turning in Reid's head as he tried to decide how best to draw out more confessions.

And what happened next, well, Jaxon blamed the altitude. Pressurized passenger compartment his ass—

when a guy was hurtling through the air six miles above the Earth, his mind didn't operate right. That was why Jaxon grabbed Reid's tie, tugged him close, and smooshed their faces together.

A kiss. God, Reid felt as good as he looked, all soft lips and solid body. And he tasted good too. Whiskey. Chocolate. Heaven. Jaxon's appetite returned in full force, but it wasn't airplane steak he was ravenous for.

Jaxon let go of the tie, but only so he could grasp Reid's shoulders instead, and Reid responded in kind. For a glorious few seconds, they made out like horny teenagers.

But before Jaxon could work out the logistics of joining the mile-high club—well, *rejoining*, since he was already a repeat member—Reid pulled away. He got off the bed and stood in the narrow space next to it, adjusting his tie. "We can't do that," he said evenly.

"Don't tell me you're not into guys, 'cause you were pretty into it." For a moment anyway.

Reid shook his head. "This is a critical mission, and I'm your assistant. I need to make sure everything goes smoothly."

"It's just a couple of concerts," Jaxon said, aware he was contradicting his earlier insistence that everything run perfectly.

"No, it's more than that."

Reid walked back into the main cabin, leaving Jaxon alone.

Chapter Four

JAXON didn't play anything else during the flight. He didn't sleep either, although he stayed on the bed, morosely watching videos on his phone. He couldn't see Reid, yet he was aware of his presence on the other side of the partial wall. Right *there*. Big as life.

When Reid appeared silently in the doorway, Jaxon gave a guilty start even though he hadn't been doing anything wrong. "We'll be landing soon," Reid said.

"Yeah, okay."

Reid sighed loudly. "Look, I know you've been briefed already, but I need to stress a few things. Remember, Vasnytsia's not like the USA. People get locked up there for all kinds of things we have the right to do at home. People disappear. You're safe—too high profile for them to fuck with—but don't push any boundaries. Please."

"I'll be a good boy."

Although he didn't look convinced, Reid nodded. "Good. And you know homosexuality's illegal, right? People who get caught are sentenced to years of hard labor."

Jaxon had already been informed of that, and the knowledge had nearly caused him to withdraw from the whole thing. Buzz had persuaded him that quitting wouldn't do Vasnytsia's gay community any good, and if Jaxon actually did the concerts, the prime minister's hard-line stance might eventually soften. Small steps, Buzz had said.

"I'm not going to fuck any Vasnytsians. I can control myself." He winced a bit as the memory of their recent kiss loomed large. "I *can*," he insisted.

"I hope so. And don't wander off on your own. We're not allowed anywhere without guides. Also, assume everyplace is bugged and someone's listening."

"Wow. It's like spy stuff, huh?" Jaxon hummed a few bars of the James Bond theme song. "Shaken, not stirred."

"This isn't a movie."

"Too bad. I always kinda wanted to act."

But since Reid looked stern and maybe slightly concerned, Jaxon relented. "I'll follow all the rules, I promise. And I'll watch what I say. No spilling state secrets—not that I know any of those to begin with."

That probably wasn't enough to satisfy Reid, but it would have to do. Soon afterward, they buckled into their seats and endured a bumpy landing.

Jaxon hadn't seen much of Starograd from the air due to heavy cloud cover, so his first real view of the city was its airport as they taxied toward the terminal. It wasn't a cheery sight. The nearly windowless building was small and drab, its white paint missing in spots and revealing the concrete walls beneath. The few other airplanes parked on the tarmac looked like military or cargo vehicles. It made sense—with travel to and from Vasnytsia severely restricted, United and Lufthansa wouldn't exactly be lining up daily flights.

Off in the distance, he spied a smudge of small high-rises, and beyond them rose a steep hill covered in trees with dark green foliage. All the colors were drab, but maybe the steel-gray sky was partly to blame.

While the plane slowed to a halt, Jaxon and Reid gathered their belongings. Reid put on his suit jacket and squared his shoulders; Jaxon gave the phone in his pocket a final pat. He'd been warned ahead of time—no cell service or Wi-Fi in this place.

The first thing he saw as he descended the stairs was a line of soldiers. Or maybe they were policemen; he couldn't tell and wasn't sure if there was a difference. They had uniforms and stern expressions, and they carried big guns. They accompanied two stout middle-aged men in dark suits and three attractive younger women. The women's suits were light blue and had skirts.

What happened next seemed to be some kind of ceremony. The soldiers saluted and then the men in suits gave speeches—in Vasnytsian, so Jaxon didn't understand a word. Reid leaned in close and translated, but that wasn't very helpful because his proximity and scent distracted Jaxon too much to pay attention. Jaxon got the gist of it anyway: *Welcome to our wonderful country. We're honored to have you here. We consider this a huge step in the friendship of our great nations.* Blah blah blah.

Jaxon gave a short speech in return, just a three-sentence lie about how honored and excited he was to be there. Reid translated that too.

The women stepped forward and introduced themselves as Jaxon's guides. They spoke excellent English, which calmed his fears a little. He didn't catch their last names, which involved more syllables and consonants than he was used to, so he hoped he wouldn't break protocol by using first names. The youngest one, a blonde, was Albina. Halyna was the one with the brunette bob. And the last one, Mariya, had long brown hair and looked like a supermodel. She batted her eyelashes at Jaxon, who might have flirted back if Reid hadn't been standing close by, thwarting any potential attractions.

The soldiers and men in suits dispersed, heading back into the terminal, but the guides came along with Jaxon and Reid. Aside from his guitar, Jaxon was traveling light; Reid even more so. As they dragged their suitcases toward a waiting SUV, the door of the plane closed and the stairway was rolled away. The jet engines were humming already. Apparently the flight crew was in a hurry to get the hell out of Vasnytsia. That was not reassuring.

The big black SUV resembled a Hummer, but Jaxon didn't recognize the brand name, which was in Cyrillic. The driver wordlessly stored the luggage in the back and then drove them out of the airport through a gate guarded by more armed soldiers. Halyna pointed out the sights. Her spiel sounded well rehearsed, but there was very little to see. Large fields of wheat surrounded the airport, and then the apartment blocks began.

Jaxon had traveled to several former communist bloc countries where he'd seen similar housing. Uniform, prefab concrete buildings seven or eight floors high, with rows of small windows set among the white or gray walls. Someone Jaxon met in Prague had referred to them as rabbit hutches. The ones in Starograd seemed to be in particularly bad repair. Many of the facades were badly cracked, and broken windows were patched with cardboard or plywood. Sad little parks ran in front of some of the buildings, with scabby-looking grass, broken benches, and pieces of scuttering litter.

The road—full of giant potholes—held very few vehicles. Most of them were military or construction trucks, although Jaxon saw a few private cars and several grungy buses. Tram tracks separated the two lanes. Although it was midmorning on a weekday, he saw very few people. Those he spied wore colorless clothing and trudged along the road or waited for trams with their heads down, plastic sacks clutched in their hands.

Large posters on walls and billboards provided some visual interest. Propaganda, Jaxon guessed. Many of them included images of a dour-looking man about Jaxon's age, wearing a fancy military uniform that dripped with medals and ribbons. Prime Minister Talmirov, no doubt. Sometimes he stared at gleaming factory machinery, sometimes he stood in a field of vegetables, and sometimes he loomed over classrooms full of schoolchildren. He never looked happy.

Halyna called attention to a depressing school and a couple of factories spewing God knew what through their chimneys into the atmosphere. The SUV rumbled past several public squares, each containing birdshit-stained statues of war heroes and edged by tram tracks. Old people and men in coveralls sat in the squares, smoking cigarettes.

The scenery improved when they reached the older part of the city. Although the buildings were in disrepair, most still possessed the ghost of past beauty. According to Halyna, some of them dated from the nineteenth century, when Vasnytsia was part of the Austro-Hungarian Empire, but many were even older, remnants of Ottoman rule.

Jaxon listened to Halyna's narration and occasionally interjected carefully polite comments. Reid remained silent, but his sharp gaze seemed to capture everything. Jaxon would have bet that Reid could give an accurate description of every block they passed. Maybe it was a holdover from his military days.

They finally arrived at what Halyna pronounced Starograd's finest hotel. Given the lack of tourism, Jaxon guessed it might be the city's only hotel. Halyna rattled off the names of famous people who'd stayed there. Jaxon recognized only a few, all of whom had died long before his parents were born.

The driver offered to help with luggage—the first time he'd spoken—but Reid told him they could manage. Halyna led them into a small lobby where two men sat in squishy chairs, staring and smoking. They wore street clothes, but something about their scrutiny convinced Jaxon they were cops or government agents. The registration desk was extravagantly carved but battered. The older woman behind it, unsmiling, handed Jaxon and Reid each a key on a tarnished metal fob.

Their adjoining rooms had a connecting door and were one floor up from the lobby. Reid's was furnished with a narrow bed, a desk and chair, a wardrobe, and a simple bathroom. Jaxon had been placed in grander quarters, a large L-shaped room containing a fair amount of furniture, including two double beds and a couch. His bathroom boasted a bidet and one of those weird European showers with a zillion sprayers and incomprehensible controls. The color scheme throughout the rooms was... interesting. Bloodred carpeting, white leather upholstery, and gold brocade curtains that looked as if they'd been stolen from impoverished minor royalty.

"Home sweet home," said Jaxon, setting his guitar on one of the beds. It wasn't a twenty-grand-per-night suite in San Francisco, but he'd slept in far worse, back in the day.

Halyna gave him a professional smile. "You will have meal now in hotel restaurant. Then we will have brief city tour."

He tried not to look impatient. "That's great, but when will I be meeting my backup band? And scoping out the venue?"

She looked puzzled, probably needing a moment to decipher his slang. Then her smile returned. "Tomorrow."

That was only a day before the first of the concerts, which wouldn't give much time for preparation. But before Jaxon could complain, Reid nodded at her. "That's fine," he said. "That'll work."

Jaxon kept his mouth closed. *Best behavior*, he reminded himself.

They ate in the hotel restaurant, a slightly claustrophobic space with fancy tablecloths and flocked wallpaper. They were the only diners. Halyna departed abruptly, leaving them to the mercies of an ancient waiter and his equally ancient assistant. Although the menus came in heavy leather cases with the choices printed on nice paper, they offered few options, and everything was in Vasnytsian. It galled that Reid had to recite the selections.

The food tasted good—a hearty tomato-based soup, bell peppers stuffed with meat and potatoes and cooked in a slightly spicy sauce, sautéed garlicky greens that looked like spinach but weren't, and some really good bread that was like a thicker version of pita bread. It was a much heavier meal than Jaxon wanted, but due to fear of causing offense, he polished it off. It came with some decent red wine, followed by tiny cups of Turkish coffee.

Reid ate all of his food but didn't drink the wine. "I like a clear head when I'm working," he explained. It was nearly the only thing he said while they ate.

Halyna collected them the minute they finished their coffee, and she whisked them back through the lobby and out the door. Jaxon would have preferred to wander on foot through the cobbled streets of the old town, but instead had to sit beside Reid in the back of the SUV.

They drove for hours, Halyna pouring Jaxon more wine as she explicated endless sites in excruciating detail. *This* was the building where Prime Minister Talmirov went to high school. *That* was the tramline he'd installed during his first year in office. *Over there* was the washing machine factory he'd personally opened last year. The three of them walked through a museum stuffed with old coins, ancient weapons, faded uniforms, and other flotsam from Vasnytsia's past. Aside from some matronly guards and one janitor with a mop, nobody else was in the building. Then they were back in the car for more slow driving past monotonous buildings. Exhausted, still full, and a little drunk, Jaxon would have fallen asleep but for Reid's subtle kicks and a strategic pinch or two.

Halyna didn't comment on the many deserted storefronts. Most people gathered in several little street markets, where sturdy women in headscarves sold food, flowers, and cheap-looking household goods. There were also a fair number of cafés where people of all ages sat at sidewalk tables with coffee, beer, and cigarettes. They stared at the SUV as it passed.

By the time they returned to the hotel, Jaxon would have sold his soul for a comfy bed. But he had to sit through dinner, again in the hotel restaurant and again alone with Reid. He ate something, but he was too exhausted to figure out what. He drank more wine.

And then finally, blessedly, he was in his room. Halyna had disappeared, and Reid stood in the connecting doorway. He still looked crisp and chipper, damn him, and somewhere along the line, he'd found a chance to shave. "Breakfast at eight," he said.

Jaxon groaned. "I don't eat breakfast."

"You will tomorrow. You need to keep your energy up."

"Ugh. I hate—" Jaxon remembered the warning about audio surveillance and shut his mouth. Then he sighed. "I just want to give good concerts, okay?"

Reid strode over and set a big hand on Jaxon's shoulder. "You will."

Weird. Just that bit of contact gave Jaxon strength and confidence. "Fine," he said. "Eight."

"Do you need an alarm?"

Jaxon pointed to the ancient LED clock next to the bed. "I don't think so."

Reid went into his own room and closed the door.

Although the bed beckoned, Jaxon felt grungy. So he spent ten cranky minutes trying to figure out the damn shower before receiving a hot but weak stream of water from one of the sprayers. He spent longer in there than he should have. Eventually, though, he emerged to complete his nighttime preparations. Then, still naked, he crawled between the bleach-scented sheets and fell asleep almost at once.

"HEY! It's past eight."

Jaxon blinked up at the giant looming over him. "Wha?"

"It's past eight. What happened to your alarm?"

"Huh? I don't— Oh." Jaxon's brain shifted sluggishly into first gear and he realized where he was. "Shit. I think I forgot to set it."

"Albina's waiting for us."

Reid stepped back as Jaxon pried himself from the bed. If Reid was scandalized by Jaxon's nudity—and morning wood—he didn't show it. But he did tilt his head and squint at Jaxon's chest. "Interesting tattoo."

Unlike many other people in the business, Jaxon hadn't covered himself in ink. He wasn't overly fond of needles, an anxiety that had probably spared him from some nasty drug addictions. But two years earlier he'd had a single large design inscribed onto the left side of his chest, directly over his heart. It was a guitar—a battered-looking acoustic—being played by a man. Although the guitar was rich in color and detail, the man was faintly sketched with black ink. He was faceless.

Jaxon patted the skin. "I was high."

"I doubt it. That's good art. Someone put a lot of time and thought into it."

It wasn't fair to have this conversation while naked and groggy. Jaxon had no defenses. "The butler at that hotel in San Francisco told me he was married to his job. I guess I'm the same. That's why I got this tattoo."

He turned and went to get ready for breakfast.

Chapter Five

ALBINA wore the same suit as the day before, or one identical to it, and her white blouse had a ridiculously large bow hanging from the collar. Her pale blonde hair was tamed in a neat ponytail, and she was aggressively perky, which annoyed the hell out of Jaxon.

"Did you enjoy your tour of our beautiful city?" she chirped as soon as he took a seat in the SUV.

He tried to think of something honest but flattering to say. "Halyna did a great job showing us around. Starograd has a lot of interesting history."

"Yes, it does. This morning I will show you more historical places."

Shit. "I thought I was going to meet with the band and see the venue. I really need to get ready for the concert."

"This afternoon," she said, her plastic smile unwavering. "This morning is more tour."

Jaxon turned to face Reid, who said, "I'm sure you'll have plenty of time to get ready this afternoon." His tone was light, but his eyes were sharp, either pleading or commanding Jaxon to concede.

And Jaxon did, although he might have been a little sulky about it. He stomped around a musty natural history museum and scowled at a statue appearing to commemorate Prime Minister Talmirov's first haircut. Then the SUV climbed the steep hill that loomed over the old city. Jaxon caught glimpses of several mansions among the trees. Albina said that back in the evil capitalist days of the late nineteenth century, these had been the homes of Vasnytsia's aristocrats and industrial barons. Today many of them housed government agencies, while others were inhabited by high-ranking officials. "It is convenient for them to access their offices this way," she said. As if that excused them reveling in luxury while everyone else squished into decaying rabbit hutches.

Near the top of the hill, the SUV stopped in front of a narrow, gated road flanked by several armed soldiers. The guards watched closely but didn't seem surprised or alarmed by their presence. They'd likely been forewarned.

"Prime minister's palace is there," Albina said, pointing, but Jaxon caught only the hint of a roofline through the trees. "I am sorry I cannot show it to you, but he is in very important meeting today."

"I'm sure he's a busy guy," Jaxon said, which was as diplomatic as he was capable of being.

"Yes. Very busy. Now we see castle."

The castle in question was at the crest of the hill, with a sweeping view of the city. It lay mostly in ruins, a sad pile of stones that only hinted at former defensive glory. Albina blamed the Ottomans, but Jaxon figured a century or more of neglect probably contributed. Still, it was a pretty location, with birds tweeting in the branches and wildflowers growing among the crumbling rocks. And it was nice to walk around outside for a short time.

"Can I take some pictures?" Jaxon asked. He'd been warned in his predeparture briefing to ask permission.

Albina nodded crisply. "Yes, please do."

Jaxon took a few shots of an intact tower and then wanted a panorama of the view. He wandered along the edge of the castle in search of the best angle. Albina and Reid stayed put near some rubble that had once been a fountain. She was speaking to him in English, but Jaxon was too far away to catch what she was saying, and Reid seemed more interested in scanning their surroundings than listening to her.

Jaxon finally found a spot where a chunk of the exterior wall had collapsed, perfectly framing the city below. He knelt on a big square rock and held up his phone, which although no help in its usual roles, still functioned fine as a camera.

Nearby sat almost the only other people at the castle, a half-dozen men and women in their early twenties. They'd been staring since he got out of the SUV, but only now was he close enough to hear them talking. Not that he could understand, since they were speaking Vasnytsian. But when he'd shifted a bit for a fresh angle, he caught one of the women saying *Jaxon Powers*. He turned to look at them and they grinned.

"Hi," he said. He would have approached them, but they all cut their eyes in Albina's direction and gave him subtle headshakes. Right. No unauthorized mixing with the locals. He nodded and tried to demonstrate with his face and posture that he wished the rules were otherwise. After checking to be sure that Albina wasn't looking at them, one of the women winked, pointed quickly at Jaxon, and then patted her chest over her heart. That small gesture meant more to him than any squealing or selfie demands.

A few minutes later, Reid strode over to join him while Albina went to the SUV to talk to the driver. "She's checking on lunch," Reid said. "Then she's promised we'll head to the venue."

"Finally."

In a quiet voice, Reid said, "You need to be patient, Jax. This mission is vital."

The patronizing tone would have irked Jaxon if not for the nickname. Hardly anyone used it. He smiled. "I'm trying."

"I know."

"Is there, um, anyone listening to us right now?"

Reid glanced around quickly. "Probably just that group over there, but I don't know if they speak English. It's not often taught here."

"They know who I am."

"You're a celebrity."

Jaxon gave his arm a gentle push. "I'm a celebrity in the free world. How does anyone here know about me if they can't get internet and stuff?"

"Information has a way of getting around barriers."

"What the fuck does that mean?"

Reid simply shrugged. Infuriating. Except... he was standing right *there*. Not touching, not even angled toward Jaxon. But all of his attention was on Jaxon, who felt it like a weight. A pleasant weight. It reminded him of the heavy quilt his grandmother wrapped around him when he was little. Jaxon was used to people focusing on him, but they were interested in Jaxon Powers, eight-time Grammy Award winner. Or maybe Jaxon Powers, a star-spangled notch on their bedposts. Few of them cared about Jax from Peril, Nebraska.

"Thanks for doing this," Reid said. "It's not your job and you could have said no."

"Sure."

"You'd be a lot happier right now tucked away in a fancy hotel suite in New York or Paris or somewhere."

Jaxon flashed him a grin. "Alone? I'm not so sure about that."

Then Albina was walking toward them and it was time to go.

LUNCH was an elaborate, heavy meal at a restaurant with gilded woodwork and velvet curtains. As he plowed through meat-filled dumplings in cream sauce, Jaxon wondered how Vasnytsians managed to stay so thin with such cuisine. Then it occurred to him that once again, he and Reid had the place to themselves— except for the waitstaff and Albina, who all hovered— and he was ashamed. He guessed that few of the locals were able to eat like this.

"Why don't you join us?" he asked Albina.

She appeared briefly startled before shaking her head. "No, no. This is for you. I eat later."

The waiters wanted to bring dessert and coffee, but Jaxon was stuffed. Besides, he felt desperate to get ready for the concert. What if the band sucked or the equipment was in the same condition as most of Starograd's buildings? He hadn't brought anything of his own, not even an electric guitar. "Can we go?" he pleaded.

Albina seemed to take pity on him and packed them back into the SUV. Jaxon hated the damned vehicle already, and he wondered if the driver was a robot. The mercifully short drive took them a hulking building with yellow paint, white columns, and a domed roof. "This is National Theatre," Albina said as the SUV came to a halt. "It was gift from Emperor Franz Joseph."

"Is he the dude who got assassinated and started World War I?"

Reid gave him an appalled look. "That was Franz Ferdinand."

"Oh, right. Like the band."

Jaxon was spared Reid's response as they got out of the car. Armed men stood at the enormous front doors of the building, but they stepped aside for Albina, who opened the door. The lobby was fancy in an overblown but faded way, with worn red carpet and marble stairs. A ceiling fresco displayed toga-clad deities playing instruments and sitting among clouds. Always a wiseass, Jaxon almost asked where Talmirov was. But then he saw him, in a poorly done rendition, playing a violin. Jaxon wondered which unfortunate god had been kicked out of the orchestra and plastered over for the prime minister's sake.

A tall, skinny man in a suit popped out of a door and came running toward them. He had a bad comb over and a thin attempt at a mustache, and he looked as if he was about to piss his pants with anxiety. He chattered at Albina and Reid so quickly that he sounded as if he was in fast-forward. When Albina introduced Jaxon, the man—whose name was Zima—shook his hand rapidly and tried to smile. Then he gestured at the group to follow him.

"Why is he so nervous?" Jaxon whispered to Reid as they walked. "Is something wrong?"

"I don't think so. He's just under pressure to make sure everything goes right."

Jaxon remembered the stories of what happened to people who displeased the Vasnytsian government, and he felt a flood of sympathy. Although Jaxon had experienced a few minor disasters in his years of performing, he'd never had to worry about being sent to the gulag.

Zima took them through several doors and down long corridors clearly not meant for public viewing, with their flickering lights, scuffed and dingy paint, and worn floor tiles. The air smelled of dust and sweat and, very faintly, of boiled cabbage.

Finally they arrived backstage, where three young men scrambled out of folding chairs to greet them. Albina and Zima did introductions, a confusing process because the drummer and bass player were both named Ivan, while the third guy, who played backup guitar and keyboards, was Igor. None of them spoke more than four words of English. Great.

Fortunately Reid and Albina could interpret, and music tended to transcend linguistic barriers. The band turned out to be familiar with Jaxon's biggest hits, also a plus. And while they weren't the most skilled musicians he'd worked with, they were acceptable. The equipment surprised Reid. Most of it appeared brand-new, probably purchased specifically for his concert. The venue was great too. Big stage, gorgeous gilded auditorium, and wonderful acoustics.

"It is okay?" Albina asked worriedly as Jaxon paced the stage.

"Yeah. It'll work out fine."

A collective sigh of relief rose to the rafters.

Jaxon stood in front of her. "So can you tell me the agenda? I know I'm supposed to play for an hour, but that's all I know." The lack of information sucked, and he still didn't understand why the plan was a state secret. Nevertheless, he'd obediently devised a set list that should satisfy Talmirov and last about sixty minutes.

"Our minister of culture himself will introduce you. Prime minister will be sitting there." She pointed to a balcony. "And then you will sing."

"No opening acts?"

She looked confused. "You will sing."

"Okay. Fine. Then what?"

"You return to hotel."

Simple enough. "And after that? I think we've covered all the tourist sights."

"Next night, we will have party at hotel. Several ministers will attend. Perhaps even prime minister himself, but he is very busy man."

With or without Talmirov, Jaxon had the impression the party wouldn't exactly be a boozy, druggy blowout. "And the second concert?"

Anxiety flooded her face. "Five nights after first concert. It is important holiday. We call it National Workers' Day. This concert will be in main square."

Jaxon didn't like outdoor concerts. For one thing, the sound carried poorly and frequently competed with other noises, such as sirens. For another, the weather was unpredictable. He'd once had to stop a summer festival gig in Missouri because a thunderstorm had rolled in, threatening to drown, electrocute, or blow everyone away. And with outdoor performances, especially free ones, crowd dynamics were tricky. The audience tended to be drunker, more hopped up on drugs, more likely to cause problems. Not that he expected the citizens of

Starograd to do a reenactment of the concert at Altamont, but the idea of this second performance still made him uneasy.

"Can't we do it somewhere else? I mean, if this place is booked, we could find another indoor location. I'm really not that picky."

Albina shook her head. "No, I am very sorry. It must be in main square." She attempted a smile. "Prime minister has invited whole city to attend."

Oh, lovely. Before Jaxon could raise a protest, Reid stepped in. "What's wrong with that venue?"

"Weather. Acoustics. Security."

"Forecast is good," Albina said. "And in any case, stage will be covered by tent. Which will help with sound also, yes?"

"A little," Jaxon admitted.

"Good. Starograd is very safe city. Not like United States. We have no guns, no crime. And also many police will be there."

Reid looked at Jaxon with concern. "Can you handle that?"

"I guess I have to," Jaxon said sourly. But he didn't have time to brood because he and the band really needed to get some practice in. Still, he scowled briefly at Reid before stalking over to pick up a guitar.

BY the time Albina informed him that practice was over, Jaxon was tired and cranky. The rehearsal itself had gone okay, and the tech guys seemed to know what they were doing. But Jaxon and the band were just getting to know each other. Even if they didn't have a language barrier, he'd have wanted to spend at least a couple more days together, working out the kinks.

"You will have dinner in hotel restaurant," Albina announced during the drive.

Jaxon groaned at the thought of more heavy food. "I'm not hungry. Couldn't I just have a sandwich in my room?"

Looking distressed, she bit her lip. "You are expected at dinner."

"But I don't—"

"We'll go," Reid interrupted. "It's fine."

It was *not* fine. Jaxon didn't want the fucking dinner. But he was also reluctant to make a scene in front of Albina and the ever-silent driver, so for the moment, an evil glare had to do.

Predictably they had the dining room to themselves. Jaxon would have fled to his room, but Reid had their keys. And Jaxon wasn't completely certain those undercover cops—or whatever they were—in the lobby wouldn't tackle him if he deviated from the plan. When Jaxon glowered and refused to even listen to the menu choices, Reid ordered for him. Humiliating. Jaxon got his revenge by not eating a single bite, even though he was aware that most Vasnytsians could only dream of food like this. And even though, well, the chicken in paprika cream sauce smelled fantastic.

Reid made a few yummy noises while eating his. Which he did incredibly slowly, as if he needed to savor every goddamn bite. After he'd cleaned his plate, he ordered chocolate cake and coffee.

Finally, when Jaxon was three seconds short of committing mayhem with a butter knife, Reid wiped his hands on the napkin and stood. Albina appeared like magic to whisk them to their rooms. Jaxon did not wish her a good night.

Alone, he rubbed his stomach. He really was a little hungry—not that he'd admit it to anyone. Maybe he had some peanuts or something in his suitcase. As he was rooting through underwear and T-shirts that he hadn't bothered to unpack, Reid burst through the connecting door.

With his jaw set, Reid grasped Jaxon's upper arm. "You're tired from practice. Time for your aqua massage."

"What?"

"Your aqua massage." As if that explained everything, Reid tugged Jaxon toward the bathroom. Jaxon would have resisted, except it was pretty damn clear Reid would win that battle. Besides, he was curious about what was up. When Reid slammed the bathroom door behind them and turned on the shower full-blast, Jaxon just waited.

Reid waited too, standing near the shower with arms crossed.

"What the hell—"

Reid shut him up with a vicious *cut* motion. Only when the mirror was thoroughly steamed up did Reid budge, but that was only to turn on the sink faucet.

"Are you trying to cause a drought?" asked Jaxon.

"I'm hoping the running water camouflages our voices. And the steam fogs up any cameras."

Alarmed, Jaxon looked around. "They have cameras in my *bathroom*?"

"Probably not. But just to be safe."

Great. Some Vasnytsian bureaucrat had the job of watching Jaxon take a shit.

"What do you want?" Jaxon demanded.

"I want you to stop acting like a spoiled child."

"I don't—"

"Complaining about the tours. Balking at the second concert. Throwing a hissy fit over dinner."

Jaxon marched closer. "It wasn't a hissy fit! I'm a professional, dammit, and I'm just trying to make sure my performances reflect that. And I'm a fully grown adult who knows when and what he wants to eat."

"Maybe. But this isn't some little show you're putting on for teenyboppers or stoned hippies. This mission is *important*. People could die if it doesn't go well. Do you understand that?"

Snarling, Jaxon moved even nearer until their chests almost touched. He wanted to shout but settled for a low growl instead, hoping the shower would drown him out. "I understand that just fine, asshole. I'm not an idiot."

"Then don't act like one."

Jaxon shoved him. Gently, but a definite shove. Of course, Reid didn't budge. Well, not at first. Then he narrowed his eyes and, with a surge of speed and power, grasped Jaxon's shoulders and propelled him backward against the closed door. Jaxon was trapped, so he attacked the only way he could. "Asshole!"

"Idiot!"

And instead of belting him, which was what Jaxon expected, Reid kissed him.

Good *Lord*. Reid's kiss was greedy, his mouth devouring as his body pressed full-length against Jaxon's. But his hands were incongruously gentle, one cradling Jaxon's skull while the fingers of the other weaved through his hair. And Jaxon was equally hungry, as if this kiss might make up for his missed meal. As if this touch might make up for what else he'd been missing. He placed his hands firmly on Reid's ass, urging tighter contact.

When Reid dragged his open mouth away from Jaxon's lips, across his cheek, and down to his neck, Jaxon groaned and tipped his head back.

He groaned again when Reid stepped away.

"I didn't mean to do that," Reid whispered. He looked slightly shocked—a man who rarely lost control.

"Yeah. Like I didn't mean to kiss you in the plane. But it was good. They were both really good kisses."

Reid nodded. "But we can't do this."

"Right. 'Cause you're my assistant."

"Because of a whole host of reasons I can't divulge."

"You have a lot of secrets." Jaxon's anger had fled completely, a fire doused by a tidal wave of lust. Now he was... sad. He was drawn so fiercely to this man who would never let him in. "You knew about the outdoor concert ahead of time, didn't you?"

Reid shifted his feet. "Not exactly. But I was fairly certain it would need a large venue, and none of the city's indoor performance spaces seat more than the National Theatre." He let his head droop briefly; when he lifted it, his expression pleaded for understanding. "For the last few years, people here have protested on National Workers' Day. We're talking thousands of people marching in the streets of Starograd, demanding government reform. Every year, the police crack down on them. Beatings, mass arrests. And then the next year, even more people show up. It's brave and... beautiful, you know?"

"What does that have to do with me?" Jaxon asked gently.

"It's mostly younger people who protest. I guess that's often the case anywhere. I think Talmirov hopes your concert will distract them—and will make them think maybe he's not such a bad guy after all."

"I'm a dictator's propaganda?"

Reid came close again, this time for a brief stroke of his fingers against Jaxon's cheek. His touch burned like fire. "I'm sorry, but yes. You'll just have to trust me that it's for a greater good."

Jaxon didn't believe in anything except music. But he promised himself he'd try to believe in Reid.

Chapter Six

JAXON remembered to set his alarm, and the next morning he ate a big breakfast without complaint. He steeled himself for more tourism, but Mariya was their guide for the day, and she seemed more interested in fashion. "What will you wear for concert tonight?" She had one of those husky voices straight men found so sexy. Under other circumstances, Jaxon would have found it sexy too.

"This." He wore a pair of skinny black jeans and a tight black T-shirt with red sleeves. It was the kind of thing he wore for all of his concerts.

She tsked. "This is not what big star should wear." And she pressed a finger against his sternum.

"People come to hear my music, not admire my outfit."

"But you are so handsome! I will find you something better."

Jaxon looked at Reid, who shrugged. After instructing Jaxon and Reid to wait in the hotel lobby, Mariya left. They sat in the squishy chairs and stared at the other two men there, who smoked and stared back. They weren't the same men Jaxon had seen when he first arrived, but every single time he passed through the lobby, two men would be seated there with cigarettes and closed-off expressions. With no sign of other guests, the men were especially obvious.

Reid leafed through one of the pamphlets from the lobby rack. They all featured Talmirov on the cover.

When Mariya returned a half hour later, she appeared excited. "I take you to tailor now. He is prime minister's personal tailor! Best in Vasnytsia."

Fantastic. But Jaxon smiled sweetly, followed her to the SUV, and was whisked to the oldest part of the city.

The tailor was a tiny man in a shop crammed with bolts of fabric, some of which, Jaxon imagined, dated from the Ottoman Empire. There were no other customers, but maybe the guy didn't need anyone else if the country's head honcho was a regular. The tailor measured Jaxon carefully and then, with Reid interpreting, got Jaxon's input on fabrics and styles. Mariya chimed in too. In the end they agreed on a black silk button-down with emerald-colored piping at the cuffs, hem, and collar. It wasn't nearly as flashy as Mariya wanted, but she gave in. She decided Jaxon's jeans were acceptable too. The tailor promised to have the shirt delivered to the theater before the concert.

On their way to the SUV, they walked for a few blocks along the pedestrian-only street and came to a café with outdoor tables. Several patrons nursed tiny cups of coffee. Jaxon turned to Mariya. "Can we please stop here for just a short time? I'd like to get a better idea of how Vasnytsians live." Not a complete lie. Mostly he wanted to fend off more sightseeing.

Although Jaxon expected resistance from his companions, Reid nodded and rested a hand on Mariya's shoulder. "He could use some relaxing time before the concert."

She clearly wasn't thrilled with this development, but after a long pause, she said, "Yes. For short time."

Jaxon wanted to kiss them both.

Mariya guided them to an outdoor table close to the café's facade, and Jaxon quickly took the outward-facing seat. Slightly rude, maybe, but he wanted to be able to see something besides her. Reid sat to his right, and Mariya settled across from Jaxon. The waiter arrived—the same model of dour, efficient server that Jaxon had seen in countless cafés and bars in Eastern Europe—and Mariya ordered Turkish coffees all around. Jaxon could decipher that much without translation.

Then they just sat there. The agenda having gone off track, Mariya didn't have a script, which clearly distressed her. So Jaxon attempted small talk. "Have you had this job for very long?"

She blinked, taken aback by a personal question, perhaps. "Since I finished school. Six years."

"You must meet some interesting people."

"Many important people wish to visit our beautiful city."

Jaxon doubted that but didn't let it show. "Are you from Starograd originally?"

"Ah, yes. We live on hill. My father is deputy minister of defense. He will be at concert tonight."

"Is he a fan?"

She laughed as if that were a really funny joke. "No. Of course all important members of government will be there."

Sounds like a fun crowd.

The waiter appeared with their drinks, and Jaxon took a careful sip of his. He loved Turkish coffee, but it was thick and bitter, and if you weren't cautious, you ended up with a mouthful of coffee grounds.

A young family sat at the table behind Mariya—father, mother, and a little boy maybe three or four years old. As the boy drew on a scrap of paper, his parents stared at Jaxon. They must have been startled to hear people speaking English. But then the woman's eyes widened, and she nudged her husband and whispered in his ear. He scrutinized Jaxon for a moment before recognition lit his gaze too; he whispered back to his wife.

Moving furtively, as if wanting to make sure nobody else noticed, the woman held her fist near her mouth and briefly mimed singing. Not wanting Mariya to notice what was going on, Jaxon risked a quick wink. That sent his little audience into a minor flurry of thumbs-upping, waving, and incomprehensible gestures. It was adorable. But then Mariya must have noticed Jaxon's attention had strayed, because she twisted around to look behind her. The couple stopped at once, the father leaning over his son's drawing and the mother staring stone-faced into her coffee.

It was sweet that Jaxon seemed to have adoring fans in Starograd, but it disturbed him that they didn't seem free to openly acknowledge that. It reminded him of being a teenager in Peril, desperate that nobody should know he liked boys even more than girls. Had he been found out, he would have faced social rejection, bullying, maybe even a beating or two. But the citizens of Vasnytsia had it worse. Disobedience regarding any of the regime's many restrictions could result in harsh imprisonment or even execution.

As he sipped his cooling coffee, Jaxon thought about change. Maybe it was cliché to say so, but things got better. At least they had for him. Nobody cared which gender he slept with. Hell, things had even improved in good old Peril. Sometimes fits of morbid curiosity hit him and he'd read the *Peril Union-Herald* online. He didn't really care who won the regional calf-roping competition or what modifications the city council made to park usage, but seeing those familiar names helped ground him. It was a much-needed reminder that he was a real human being, not just a brand name.

Two or three years ago, he'd been thrilled to find an article about the winter dance at Peril High. One of his first public performances had been at that dance. Photos with the article showed kids dressed up and smiling, eating, talking. But what truly caught his attention was a picture of the dance floor—where a pair of boys in suits held each other tightly in a slow dance. None of the other kids were paying them any attention; they were too caught up in their own dancing. The article didn't mention the boys either.

Maybe if the people of Peril could be nonchalant about a gay couple at a high school dance, there was hope for Vasnytsia too.

JAXON didn't know whether the café stop meant Mariya had to cancel a visit to a dusty museum or more circling in the SUV. But after they finished their coffees, she had the driver take them straight to the theater, which was excellent as far as Jaxon was concerned. The band waited there, fussing with their instruments. Jaxon spent several hours practicing with them, doing sound checks, and having complicated translated discussions with the light and sound guys. He always loved preparing for a performance, and this was no exception. Reid proved a capable assistant, not just interpreting when needed but also making sure Jaxon was kept supplied with bottles of water.

To Jaxon's delight, assistants carried in a lunch of sandwiches and fruit, a welcome respite from the heavy fare he'd been forced to eat since he arrived. But the way Ivan One, Ivan Two, Igor, and the crew fell on the food made him wonder how often they went hungry. Or at least how rarely somebody else picked up the tab.

Late in the afternoon, Jaxon finished his fifth rendition in a row of "Lightning Bugs," one of his biggest hits. It was a jaunty tune with a slower bridge and finale, and although the words were about childhood summers, the song also conjured the loss of innocence and the bittersweet sense of growing older. Ivan Two, the bass player, hadn't quite caught the right mood yet; he wavered between funereal and rockabilly. So Jaxon demonstrated one more time and then waited while Ivan One and Igor—who'd caught on some time ago—tried to coach their compatriot. Just as Jaxon was about to launch into the sixth round, Reid stood in front of him.

"You need to take a break, Jax."

"Later. Ivan's still—"

"He's close. He can keep practicing. You need to save your voice and energy for tonight."

Reid was right, but Jaxon didn't admit it out loud. Instead he unstrapped his guitar and set it on the stand. "Are we going back to the hotel?"

"No. It's not worth it since it's an early show. But you have a dressing room to yourself."

That would have to do. On the bright side, it would keep Mariya from making him tour a factory or eat more meat-butter-cheese-cream-flour concoctions. Jaxon nodded at the Ivans and Igor before following Reid backstage.

Unlike the public spaces in the theater, the dressing room wasn't plush or grand. It held a white leather couch that looked identical to the one in his hotel room, a dressing table, and a few chairs. An ancient TV—the kind in a huge wooden case—squatted on a stand in the corner, its screen dark. Whatever color the walls had once been, they had now faded to a sickly yellow. But there were bottles of water and a couple of bowls of shelled nuts, and the room was blessedly quiet. Jaxon collapsed onto the couch.

"Do you want me to stand in the hallway and make sure nobody disturbs you?" Reid asked.

"Could you stay in here instead?"

"Sure." Reid grabbed two water bottles. He handed one to Jaxon and then pulled out a chair so it blocked the closed door. He sat and drained half his bottle in one go. "You doing okay?"

"Yeah, sure. It's not a bad setup. I wish I'd had more time with the band, but…." He shrugged philosophically.

"It'll be a select crowd tonight. Tickets by invitation only, and most of them went to government officials and their families."

Mindful of the likely presence of cameras or bugs, Jaxon simply nodded.

After a pensive moment, Reid squinted at him. "It's a big deal that you're here, you know. You're the first non-Vasnytsian to perform in this theater in… well, a long time."

Jaxon didn't feel honored. He felt burdened and used, a trained monkey trotted out to appease a tyrant and mollify his constituents. But Jaxon's own government was using him too. And while he was in favor of democracy, world peace, and all those good things, he wasn't convinced these stupid concerts would help achieve any of it. He was just a token in an endless game. He was the damned thimble on the Monopoly board—and hadn't they recently gotten rid of the thimble?

He set the bottle of water aside, unopened. "I'm tired." He scooted around so he lay on the couch with his feet hanging over the end, and he closed his eyes.

"Do you want me to go?"

"No." Jaxon opened his eyes and turned his head to see Reid. "Just turn out the lights, okay?"

"Sure."

The room went dark except for the thin band of light under the door. It wasn't bright enough for Jaxon to see anything, but he heard Reid breathing. More importantly, he *felt* Reid sitting just a few strides away, a watchful presence even when he couldn't see.

"What do you think of my music?" Jaxon asked. "Honestly."

"I think you're incredibly talented."

"Yeah, okay. But what about the songs?"

Reid didn't answer immediately. Jaxon was okay with not seeing his face, because Reid's expression would, as usual, have given nothing away. Darkness seemed more honest. "I think," Reid said slowly, "your songs are your soul. I think that even when they seem as if they don't mean anything important, that's not the case. Every word and every note is a true piece of you. I think that's why you have so many fans. Not because you're pretty and your melodies are catchy, but because when people listen, they know you're genuine. You're real."

Jaxon found it hard to breathe. He'd read a lot of reviews of his work over the years, received a lot of compliments and fan mail. But nobody had ever acknowledged that his music was *him*.

"But do you like them?" he asked.

Another long pause. "They're not my style. Not my usual genre, I guess." Reid chuckled. "I like the Beatles. But your songs... the more I hear them, the more I like them. Maybe they could be my style. Someday."

Oddly comforted, Jaxon drifted into sleep.

Chapter Seven

REID woke him with a gentle tap on the shoulder an hour before the show. Jaxon had dreamed of crumbling castles and men with guns, and the nap had done little to refresh him. But he got himself ready, including putting on the newly delivered shirt. It fit perfectly and, admiring himself in the mirror, he had to admit he looked really good. Better than in a T-shirt.

"Do you want to stay in here all night?" Reid asked, looking amused. "I can ask them to put a mirror onstage if that will help."

"If you were about to be stared at by hundreds of people for an hour, you'd care how you looked too." Except Reid always looked great, damn him. Even after hours of schlepping around Starograd, his suit was neat, his shirt crisp, and his tie knotted just right. He always looked as if he'd stepped right off the page of a magazine ad. He probably looked great even when he was just out of bed—naked and barely awake.

And that sent Jaxon's mind to places it shouldn't go.

The Ivans and Igor seemed nervous and smelled like booze, but they managed the sound check just fine. Then the crew did some last-minute fussing with amps and lights and the mixer board. Instead of using in-ear monitors, the theater had onstage loudspeakers for Jaxon and the band. It was an old-fashioned approach, but Jaxon had done it before and didn't mind. On the other side of the heavy curtains, the sounds of a gathering crowd were evident, and Jaxon imagined a theater full of men in uniforms and women in suits, each man a clone of Talmirov and each woman a variation of Albina, Halyna, or Mariya.

Reid paced slightly backstage—the closest to anxiety Jaxon had seen from him—but he managed an encouraging smile. "Do you need anything?"

"Just keep some water handy. I'll signal you if I need some. Oh, and when we're done here? My throat's gonna be pretty raw. If you could arrange for tea with honey and lemon to be waiting at the hotel, that would be great. Add some rum and it's even better."

"Rum's unlikely. Will vodka do?"

"Sure, why not?"

Then Zima scurried over and said something.

"Time?" Jaxon asked.

Reid nodded. "Break a leg."

Jaxon never experienced stage fright. As a kid he'd been awkward, the type to skulk around the edges of social gatherings and spend his lunches alone. Part of that had come from the early realization that he was different from his peers, but part of it was just him. He wasn't great at peopling. Not even now, really. He was fine with fans and had no problem finding someone to hook up with, but conversations could be painful if he wasn't high on something.

Despite all that, he was perfectly comfortable when he stepped onto a stage. Shine the lights on him? Stick a mic in his hand? Make him the focus of thousands of eyes? All perfectly good. In his personal life, he was a graceless man. Onstage he was a fish in water, a snake shedding its old skin, a lion surveying his kingdom. He was fully himself.

Jaxon and the band exchanged a round of thumbs-ups. Then he took his spot behind the mic stand and waited, but not for long. The curtains crept open.

Despite the lights in his eyes, Jaxon could make out what seemed to be a full house, the audience older than his usual fans, the men well dressed in suits or uniforms, and the women in dresses. A lot of watchful-looking men stood against the walls, some with guns slung over their shoulders. Jaxon decided to ignore them.

A recorded orchestral swell poured from the speakers and cut through the silence. Everyone scrambled to their feet and sang along with what Jaxon assumed was the national anthem. He just stood there and tried to look respectful. A man with a ridiculous mustache and an impressive potbelly strode onstage for a short speech. He bowed to Jaxon when he was finished, then exited.

As an honest-to-God fanfare blasted through the auditorium, everyone rose to their feet again. A slight rustling occurred backstage, and then Jaxon got his first in-person view of Prime Minister Talmirov, dressed in a military uniform heavily festooned with medals and ribbons. Talmirov, despite his straight back and

assertive stride, was quite a bit shorter than he appeared
in the propaganda. When he reached Jaxon, Talmirov
smiled broadly before grasping his hand and giving it
a firm shake. "Very pleased to meet you," he said in a
voice not meant to carry. Although he was smiling, his
gaze was hard, cold, and calculating.

"Thank you for inviting me," Jaxon replied,
because Best Behavior. "I was happy to learn I have
such an eminent fan."

Looking pleased, Talmirov gave a minuscule bow.
Then he took the mic and gestured at the crowd to sit down.
While they were obeying, Albina showed up onstage
in the type of sparkling tight gown usually reserved for
game-show hostesses. She took her place beside Jaxon
and quietly interpreted Talmirov's speech.

The speech didn't really need translating; Jaxon
could have guessed its main content. Lots of bullshit
about how wonderful Vasnytsia was, how strong a
nation, and how super cool that a huge star like Jaxon
Powers wanted to perform here. Jaxon wondered whether
Talmirov wrote that crap himself or had a minister of
malarkey do it for him. In any case the audience ate it up,
staring in adoration and clapping wildly.

Jaxon was relieved when Talmirov nodded regally
at him and swept off the stage.

That was Jaxon's cue to begin playing, and he
plunged directly into a song about a farmer who feared
his crops would fail. Metaphor, sure, but it had been
a huge hit early in his career, and Jaxon thought it
appropriate for this country, whose economy relied
largely on agriculture. When he'd added the song to the
playlist, he wondered what would happen if some of the
farmers from Peril met their Vasnytsian counterparts.
Would they have the same things to complain about—

the weather, commodity prices, the cost of equipment, difficulties finding good labor, stupid government policies? At least none of that criticism would get the Nebraskans tossed into jail.

Now, though, those thoughts were far away. As he coaxed the chords from his guitar and the words from his throat, he *was* that farmer—a man desperately worried about his future and blaming himself for bad decisions while trying to keep his cool around family and friends. That man was angry too, and frustrated and sad, yet he held just enough hope to keep going on.

When Jaxon sang, the audience became his confidant. They were the type of friend who would listen to his thoughts and feel his emotions, yet never judge him harshly.

The audience clapped when the song was done, but he segued straight into the next one. This tune was newer, written five years before. It was about a woman who'd died from an overdose, and each stanza was from the point of view of someone she'd left behind—her lover, her child, her mother, her best friend, her drug dealer. The final verse was in the voice of the medical examiner who'd performed her autopsy.

The band kept up with him, and Ivan the drummer was excellent. They all sailed through the music, tearing through the faster pieces and taking their time with the slow. At last they came to the final tune, "Dance One More for Me." It had a retro-punk feel with slightly melancholy lyrics, and he almost always closed his sets with it. Not just because it was one of his most popular hits, but also for what it said to the audience in its plea: *Don't leave me yet. I'll be so alone when you're gone.*

After the final echoes faded away, a strange hush fell over the theater. Every eye was trained on the balcony where Talmirov sat. Once Talmirov stood and began to clap, the auditorium nearly shook with the sound of the audience joining in.

Jaxon had been instructed not to do an encore. So instead he bowed, first to the audience and then to the band. He waved at the tech guys, who'd done a good job. "Thank you," he said into the ebbing ovation. He set the guitar on its stand and walked backstage.

After that, everything was fuzzy. Jaxon knew a lot of musicians who were all keyed up after a performance, who wanted to party until they passed out. But not him. After a concert, he felt fragile and empty, like a man recovering from a bad fever. He'd once chatted with a guy who was into BDSM, and when the guy told him about sub drop—the feelings of temporary fatigue and depression he'd get after a scene—Jaxon had immediately understood.

Usually Buzz was there to collect Jaxon, or he'd send someone he trusted. Sometimes that someone might be willing to sleep with Jaxon too, because sex helped a little. But tonight Reid was there with a water bottle in hand. He gave it to Jaxon. "Good? Or do you want something harder?"

"Just want to sleep." Jaxon slurred the words slightly.

Reid managed to clear a path through the backstage people and ushered Jaxon out of the theater through a back door. One of their guides accompanied them, but Jaxon was too blurred to notice which one. He could barely remember their names anyway. Right now he could hardly remember his own.

In the back seat of the SUV, he slumped against the window and thought about nothing at all.

A large pot of hot tea waited on a tray in his hotel room, along with a sliced lemon and a jar of honey.

"You found rum," he said when he spied the small bottle near the teapot.

"Mariya found it for me. She got the tea too. It has some herbs that are supposed to be good for sore throats."

"Great."

Jaxon sat on the white leather couch and watched dully as Reid prepared a mug of tea, complete with a healthy shot of booze. Reid handed him the drink, then sat beside him. Although Jaxon burned his tongue on the first sip, he kept on drinking. Whether it was the herbs or the honey, lemon, or rum, the concoction soothed nicely as it went down.

"Was Talmirov happy?" Jaxon asked after a while.

"Word is he was thrilled."

"Okay."

"Jax—"

"I don't want to hear what a fab patriot I am. Not now." Jaxon angled himself away from Reid.

"That's not what I was going to say." Reid paused. When he continued, his voice was hushed. "I've never seen anyone as naked as you were on that stage. I had no idea before tonight what courage it must take to perform."

Jesus. In his current condition, Jaxon was likely to burst into tears. He swallowed the rest of the tea quickly and set the mug on the table. "I'm gonna crash."

"Do you want dinner?"

Ugh. "No. Not now. Maybe later?"

"I'll make sure something's available if you need it. And there's nothing scheduled for tomorrow until the banquet, so sleep as late as you want."

"Good. Thanks."

Not caring that Reid was watching, Jaxon stood and began shedding clothes. He kept on his boxer briefs and crawled into bed. He wished he had someone to share it with, even if only for the night. Reid's voice came from across the room. "I'll be next door if you need anything."

"Okay."

The lights clicked off, and the door closed with a soft thud.

IF Jaxon dreamed, he remembered nothing. He glanced at the alarm clock and was surprised to discover it wasn't even midnight. By the time he found a light switch and shambled to the bathroom, he realized he was starving. After pissing and washing his face, he poured a mug of tea from the barely tepid teapot and gulped it down. Still wearing nothing but his underwear, he opened the connecting door to Reid's room.

Reid and Mariya sat on a love seat, their bodies so close she was practically on his lap. She was fully dressed, but he'd taken off his jacket and tie and rolled up the sleeves of his pale blue dress shirt. Mariya's hand rested cozily on his upper arm, her mouth almost touching his ear.

Both of them moved only their heads when Jaxon took a step into the room. They stared at him, and Reid looked angry. "Jaxon—"

"You're still awake, I see. Good for you." Voice steady and cool as the Nebraska Sandhills in January. "I'm hungry."

Mariya stood and smoothed her skirt, then straightened her hair. "I brought some food."

"Of course you did. You're a helpful lady."

That made Reid glare, but Jaxon ignored him, just as Mariya pretended not to notice Jaxon's underwear. She crossed the room to the desk, where three dome-covered plates sat, lifted the covers, and set them aside. "Do you want some as well?" she asked Reid.

"No."

She handed one of the plates to Jaxon, who remained just inside the door. "It is special food from village in eastern part of country. We call it—"

"I don't care what it's called." He bit into a hot dog–shaped piece of baked phyllo dough filled with a mixture of vegetables and minced meat. "Great," he said with his mouth full. "Delish. You kids have a good night, now."

Without another glance at Reid, Jaxon stomped into his own room. Yeah, he slammed the door—but who cared? It wasn't as if he'd disturb any other guests.

Standing in the center of the floor and defiantly getting crumbs all over the carpet, Jaxon ate. Under ordinary circumstances, the food might have been tasty, but tonight it was dry and bitter. Despite that, he ate it all.

He was just debating whether to set the plate on a table or hurl it at the wall when the connecting door flew open. Jaxon wasn't entirely surprised when Reid rushed in, grabbed his arm, and dragged him toward the bathroom, dish and all.

"Where's Mariya?" Jaxon asked as they moved.

"Shut up."

In the bathroom, Reid slammed the door, turned on the shower, and snatched the plate away. When he set the dish on the toilet lid, it clattered loudly but didn't break.

"What's *your* problem?" Jaxon demanded. "I wasn't the one breaking the no-fraternizing rule."

"I wasn't fraternizing," Reid snapped.

"Yeah? So what do you call it? Snuggling? Canoodling? Networking? Fucking your way to world peace?"

"We weren't fucking!"

"Not yet," Jaxon said sweetly. "And you know what? If you're going to be running all that water anyway, I'm going to use it. I reek." He stepped out of his underwear and into the shower. He yelped—Reid had set the control on cold—but by now Jaxon had figured out how to work the damn thing, and he twisted the knob to warmer.

Reid yanked open the shower door. "You're being childish."

"I'm taking a fucking shower."

"I'm trying to do my job and you're throwing tantrums."

"I thought your job was assisting *me*!" Jaxon shouted. Then he stood completely under the stream, the better to ignore Reid.

Except it was hard to ignore Reid when he stepped—shoeless but otherwise fully clothed—into the shower and got right up in Jaxon's face. "I am assisting you. And I'm protecting you. You have no fucking idea how much is at stake here. You don't know what's going on!"

"Maybe that's because you won't tell me!"

"I *can't* tell you!"

"Right. Because I'm nothing but a stupid, bratty singer." Jaxon spun around to face the shower controls. But as he reached for the soap, Reid grasped his shoulders and gently urged him to turn back.

"You're not nothing," said Reid, his voice barely carrying over the sound of the water. The anger had drained from his face, replaced by something different, a complex emotional mixture that Jaxon couldn't decipher.

When Reid let go of Jaxon's shoulders and used his thumbs to smooth droplets away from Jaxon's eyes, something broke inside of Jaxon. He threw himself against Reid—which proved to be an unwise decision on a slippery shower floor. They tumbled together, landing in a tangle with Reid mostly on top. Instead of scrambling to get away, Reid kissed him.

This third time was definitely the charm. Heedless of the water drenching them, Jaxon joined in the kiss while attempting to pull off Reid's sodden clothing. At the same time, he held Reid firmly so he wouldn't get cold feet and pull away.

Luckily Reid seemed in no mood to go anywhere. He proved remarkably agile, managing to tear off his shirt and rid himself of trousers and briefs, all without breaking contact with Jaxon's mouth. Maybe they were maneuvers he'd picked up in the military.

Oh God, as beautiful as Reid looked in his tailored suits, he was even more gorgeous naked, his wet skin glistening over firm muscles. And as wonderful as he looked, he felt even better. In contrast to his solidity, his caresses were gentle, as if even in his impassioned state, he was wary of the damage his hands could do.

The tile felt unforgivingly hard, and Jaxon was at risk of drowning or being crushed, but all that mattered was the taste of Reid's tongue, the feel of his strong ass under Jaxon's palms, and the feral little growls he made when they stopped kissing long enough to breathe. Jaxon wanted more of him; he wanted to engulf and be engulfed. As they thrust hard against each other, trying for more friction despite the water, Reid dragged his mouth down Jaxon's neck and across his collarbone, then to his shoulder. He was stroking Jaxon's chest and face with poor aim but much delicacy—and then he bit.

That was it. That one extra piece of sensory input caused Jaxon's body to take over as his higher brain functions shut down completely. He howled as he climaxed.

Shower floors weren't made for cuddling. Reid and Jaxon disentangled and climbed out, leaving the water running. Then they stood for a moment, staring at each other. They were both soaking wet, Reid's eyes wide, his lips kiss-swollen, his cock still half-hard. And he was wearing sodden dress socks.

Jaxon started to giggle, which turned into a full-blown laugh, and then into such hard guffaws that he collapsed, his bare ass on the cold tile floor. Reid stared down at him with hands on hips, which only made Jaxon laugh harder. By the time he caught his breath, he was flat on his back, a Reid-thrown towel draped over his chest.

"Are you okay?" Reid asked.

Fearing another eruption of laughter if he replied, Jaxon only nodded. He took Reid's offered hand, levered himself to his feet, and dried off while Reid watched silently. "Aren't you going to say something about this being a bad idea?" Jaxon asked.

"Kind of late for that."

"Is it, though? A bad idea?"

"Phenomenally." Reid sighed, stepped closer, and stroked Jaxon's cheek. "Can't say I regret it, though." And then he shocked Jaxon by gathering him into an embrace and resting his head on Jaxon's shoulder.

Jaxon could have stayed like that forever. But he suddenly noticed a small round bandage stuck to Reid's left bicep. "What's this?" he asked, touching it gently.

Reid flinched. "Just... nothing. A cut."

"How the hell do you cut yourself there?"

"I dunno. Just did."

Jaxon would have liked to pursue the matter, but he doubted he'd get a straight answer. And he didn't want to get into another argument, partly because he lacked the energy for a second round of sex. Another night, perhaps.

"I need to get some sleep." He gently pulled out of the embrace and put on his briefs. His hair was a mess, and he'd never quite gotten around to soaping or shampooing, but he could shower again in the morning. If there was any water left in Starograd.

Reid put on his wet clothes, which must have looked damned strange if any cameras were watching. He turned off the shower, picked up the plate from the toilet seat, and followed Jaxon into the main room. "Do you need anything?" Reid asked. "There's food left. Or I could order more tea."

"No, thanks. I just need to crash." Jaxon made his way to the bed. "Don't wake me up for breakfast, okay?"

"Okay."

Reid walked toward the connecting door. As he was reaching for the knob, Jaxon called his name and Reid turned around.

"I don't regret it either," Jaxon said.

Smiling, Reid gave a small salute, entered his own room, and closed the door softly.

Jaxon turned off the lights and climbed between the sheets. He'd told the truth—he didn't regret what they'd just done. But he was miserable with the suspicion that they'd never do it again.

Chapter Eight

IT was glorious to sleep in, unmolested by alarm clocks or guides who insisted he eat a huge breakfast. But Jaxon's stomach was growling by the time he finished showering—this time solo, with soap and shampoo—and got dressed. He knocked on the connecting door.

"Come in," Reid answered at once. Jaxon half expected to find him cozying up with Mariya again, but Reid was alone. Wearing a suit, he sat in an armchair with a paperback in his hands.

"What are you reading?" Jaxon asked as he entered.

Reid held up the book, but the title was in what Jaxon presumed was Vasnytsian. "Albina brought it for me. It's a history of the country."

"Learning anything new?"

"It's a different perspective from what I got back home. Did you know Vasnytsia has a 100 percent literacy rate?"

"Uh, no."

"Tied with North Korea for highest in the world." Reid stuck a piece of paper into the book to mark his place before closing it. "Did you sleep well? How's your throat?"

"Yes and fine. You can tell Mariya her herbs worked wonders. In fact, I'd love to know what they were."

Reid stood. "You can ask her yourself at the banquet."

"Oh, yeah. That's tonight." Jaxon crossed the room and looked out the window. While his room had two large bay windows with views of the river that snaked through the old part of the city, Reid's view was of a narrow alley.

After staring at the cobblestones for a minute or two, Jaxon turned around. "I'm hungry. Do you think we could eat somewhere besides the hotel?"

"I'll find out." Reid picked up the room phone, poked at the buttons, and had a short conversation in Vasnytsian. He was grinning when he hung up. "Our guide will be with us shortly."

"Are they staying in the hotel? Or do they just skulk here when we're in our rooms?"

"Skulking, I think. The front desk staff knows how to contact them."

"Okay."

They waited. They couldn't say anything too honest, couldn't stand too close, couldn't let on to any potential audience that they were anything but a rock star and his assistant. Yet oddly, no awkwardness hung between them. Reid had said he had no regrets, and in the stark light of day, Jaxon believed him.

Halyna arrived minutes later, her hair perfectly arranged in its bob, her pale yellow blouse sporting an oversize bow. Did the guides have any say as to what they wore? Was it officially a uniform or just a very specific dress code?

"You want to go somewhere to eat?" she asked, looking puzzled. "Hotel restaurant is not good?"

"No, it's great. I just wanted to try something different. Maybe a place where the locals eat?"

"Most people eat at home. Restaurants are expensive." It was the first time she'd acknowledged that life in Starograd wasn't all rainbows and kittens, and she looked guilty when she said it.

"I understand," he said. "I'm from this little town where there were hardly any restaurants. For a lot of folks, going out was a big deal. Special occasions only." His family had enjoyed a little more money than average in Peril, but they'd had to budget tightly too. "If I wanted a treat at the Dairy Queen, I had to earn the money myself."

Her professional mask slipped just a bit as she gazed at him. For the first time, he had the feeling he was seeing the real Halyna and not a government-mandated facade. "One moment, please," she said eventually. "I will make phone call." She left them alone in the room.

"We had a DQ too," Reid said. "It was two blocks from the library. A good Saturday for me was a couple of hours at the library and then a chocolate-dipped cone on the way home."

Reid had spoken so little about his background in general, and his childhood specifically, that these statements took Jaxon by surprise. He would have pictured young Reid spending his weekends playing baseball, football, or whatever sport was in season, not hiding among bookshelves.

But before Jaxon had the chance for follow-up questions, a grinning Halyna was back with a slightly wicked gleam in her eyes. "We will go out," she announced.

The SUV took them away from the old part of the city, past the newer commercial buildings, to the part of Starograd dominated by ugly apartment buildings and belching factories. The driver stopped at one of the apartments, and although he was as silent as always, something about the way he gripped the steering wheel suggested disapproval.

Like many other buildings, this one housed a few small businesses on the ground floor: a bakery, a tiny grocery, a shoe repair place, and a restaurant. Halyna paused outside the door to the latter. "Larger factories have canteens to feed workers. It is part of their salary, yes? But some smaller factories do not, so workers eat at places like this one. We call them potato kitchens. Food is plain, but very cheap and healthy."

"Oh, like Polish milk bars," said Jaxon. When both Halyna and Reid looked at him in surprise, he shrugged. "I do travel, you know. A lot. And I don't just hang out in Michelin-starred restaurants." Actually, he'd learned about milk bars after a concert in Krakow, years ago, when he'd hooked up with a handsome university student and spent three days drinking vodka and prowling eateries.

Halyna opened the door for them. Not surprisingly, the interior smelled like potatoes, cabbage, and onion. The décor reminded him of his high school cafeteria: long tables with attached backless benches, a scuffed white floor, and pale green walls with a few posters tacked up. Except the posters in high school had featured the food pyramid instead of Bogdan Talmirov. Only a few customers sat on the benches, most of them younger men in coveralls, all of them openly staring.

With Halyna leading the way, Jaxon and Reid walked to the counter separating the kitchen from the dining area. Several unsmiling women in white coats were chopping food or washing dishes, but one of them came over to take their order. Of course Jaxon could neither read the simple menu posted overhead nor understand the conversation, so he had to trust Reid and Halyna to choose wisely. Soon the worker gave each of them a metal tray loaded with dishes, and Halyna handed a few coins to the cashier. The three of them sat at an empty table.

"So what am I eating?" asked Jaxon. He pointed. "I got this one—shredded carrots. But the rest?"

Halyna answered. "Dumplings with farmer cheese and greens. Potato… I do not know what it is called in English. Potatoes fried with onions."

"Hash browns, sort of. Okay. And the soup?"

"More potatoes and cabbage. And, er, pork."

Jaxon raised his eyebrows. "You sound a little uncertain about that."

"No, it is pig. But… this soup uses, er, leftover bits. Feet, head, uh…." She rubbed somewhere near her belly. "Sorry. I do not know word in English." She said something in Vasnytsian.

"Liver," Reid translated helpfully. But he looked wary, as if expecting Jaxon to throw a fit.

Instead, Jaxon took a big spoonful. A little bland, maybe, but not bad. When he took another swallow, not only did Reid and Halyna visibly relax, but all of the watching customers broke into grins. A few even raised their thumbs at him.

"You like?" Halyna asked.

"Yeah. I bet it's great when the weather's cold."

"I thought Americans do not eat leftover bits."

He swallowed his soup and speared a dumpling. "Some do. It depends where people are from, where their family's from. But look, I understand that eating practices differ from place to place. I've visited countries where poor people eat whatever they can get their hands on, and I've been to lots of places where nobody wants to waste anything. Anyway, I figure if I'm willing to eat the rest of the pig, I shouldn't get grossed out by its tongue or feet or whatever."

Halyna was nodding. "Yes, it is wrong to waste when some go hungry."

At that point they all dug into their meal in earnest, the tin cutlery clattering pleasantly against the chinaware. Halyna asked questions about some of the other places Jaxon had visited—the first time she'd shown interest in the rest of the world. He told her about seeing bears in Alaska and dolphins in Hawaii, and the time he got drunk in Cambridge, England, attempted to punt a boat, and ended up falling in the River Cam. She oohed and aahed and laughed, and he fully realized how young she was. Did she yearn for the opportunity to see the world outside of Vasnytsia? He didn't ask.

Reid remained mostly silent as they ate, his inscrutable expression firmly in place. But a flame blazed in his eyes, making Jaxon burn whenever he glanced Reid's way.

They finished their lunch with cups of Turkish coffee.

"Would you like to see more Starograd now?" Halyna asked.

"Thanks, but what I'd really like to do is relax in my room." A song had germinated in the depths of his brain, and he wanted to urge it to grow.

"Okay."

Jaxon stood and, following the example of other customers who'd completed their meals, took the trays of empty dishes to a rack at the far end of the restaurant. Everyone smiled as he passed. And when he returned, he realized some of them were very quietly humming one of his songs.

A tall young man in gray coveralls whispered when Jaxon reached him. "Jaxon Powers!"

Although Jaxon didn't want to get anyone in trouble, he couldn't resist a quick stop. So he knelt and pretended to fuss with his shoelace. "Hi!" he whispered back.

"My friends, we listen to your songs every night at Black Cat Café. You are very good."

Jaxon risked a quick grin. "Thank you!" Then he winked, stood, and returned to Reid and Halyna.

BACK at the hotel, Halyna said she'd collect them for the banquet. And then she disappeared. Jaxon imagined his guides in a secret break room equipped with an alarm, should he attempt to leave without them. But he didn't go anywhere. Instead he sat on the couch with his guitar—a notepad next to him—coaxing the new tune into reality.

Although Reid had offered to go to his own room, Jaxon sensed his reluctance and asked him to stay. Reid sat in an armchair with his book, seemingly engrossed in reading, yet sometimes Jaxon saw his toe tapping in time with the music.

Composing with someone else nearby was unusual, but Jaxon discovered he liked it. When a particular riff came out especially well, Reid would show the ghost of a smile. And although Jaxon wrote the words rather than singing them, they flowed more easily in Reid's presence.

After a couple of hours had passed, Jaxon set aside the guitar and stood to stretch.

"Taking a break?" Reid asked.

Jaxon smiled. "Nope. I'm done. I finished the song." He felt the happy fullness in his soul that meant he'd created something good.

"Can I hear it?"

"Nope."

Reid frowned at him. "Why not?"

"Because you're not the only one who can keep a secret. I'll play it later." But since Jaxon wasn't trying to annoy Reid, he diverted the conversation. "I think I have fans here. Aside from the prime minister, I mean. How does that happen?"

Reid glanced around as if expecting surveillance equipment to suddenly become visible. Then he shrugged. "Told you. Information has a way of traveling, when it's worthwhile information."

"I'm worthwhile?"

"Yes."

Jaxon paced the length of the room a few times. "I need some exercise."

"I can call Halyna—"

"I don't want a tour. Just sweating."

Reid ended up calling Halyna anyway, and she revealed that the hotel had a fitness center. Hallelujah. When Reid mentioned that neither of them had workout gear, she promised to dig something up right away.

Thirty minutes later she delivered two fairly ugly but serviceable tracksuits, in the correct sizes no less, and a pair of running shoes for Reid. Jaxon had brought his own.

The fitness center turned out to be a claustrophobic space in the basement, equipped with an ancient treadmill, a decent set of weights, and a third machine Jaxon didn't recognize. It seemed more geared toward torture than exercise.

"We look like we're on a team together," Jaxon said, gazing at their dual reflections in the mirror. Their tracksuits matched, red piped with gray.

Reid grinned. "We are."

Jaxon took command of the treadmill while Reid lifted weights. That was more than a little distracting; several times Jaxon nearly tripped over his own feet. Reid finished first and then watched Jaxon run. "You're fast," he observed.

Jaxon just panted through a grin. He'd always been a good runner.

When they returned to their rooms, Jaxon hopped into his shower. He couldn't help but recall what had happened there the previous night, and he jacked off quickly, like a teenager afraid of being caught by his parents.

Although Jaxon hated suits, he'd been told to pack at least one, and he'd complied—sort of. His wasn't the conservative navy-colored slacks and jackets Reid favored. Instead Jaxon had brought the outfit from last year's Grammys: blue slacks with bold gray pinstripes and a matching jacket and waistcoat with a low-cut front. No shirt, which meant much of his chest was bare and quite a lot of his tattoo was visible. His shiny black boots sported high stacked heels.

He didn't shave, but he did spend some time fussing with his hair, including applying a judicious amount of product. Then he examined himself critically in the mirror. He looked like a rock star, not some kid from Nebraska. Today he wasn't sure if that pleased him.

When Reid caught sight of him, an eyebrow flew up. "Wow."

"Impressed wow or judgmental one?"

"Surprised. But also impressed. You look great." Reid looked down at himself as if suddenly doubting his own look. Which he shouldn't have, because he was as delicious as always.

"I don't really dress up all that often. I used to, back when I first made it big. I had a bunch of money burning a hole in my pocket, and all those designer threads were so shiny compared to the polyester and denim my parents used to buy me from Svoboda Ranch and Home."

The corner of Reid's mouth turned up. "Peril's not a hotbed of high fashion?"

"That depends on how you feel about Wrangler jeans and Justin boots." Jaxon shrugged. "But you know what? I'm most comfy in jeans and a tee. So that's what I usually stick to. I bet you were born in a suit."

Reid's expression darkened. "No, I wasn't. You ready to go?"

"I guess so."

Halyna collected them soon after. She wore a slinky evening gown the color of a summer sky, but her smiles seemed brittle.

"Is something wrong?" Jaxon asked as she led them down the hotel hallway.

"No, of course not. Everyone is ready. It is excellent banquet."

"Will the prime minister be there?" Reid's face didn't show whatever he hoped the answer would be.

"No," she said. "He is very busy. He sends his regrets to Mr. Powers."

Jaxon nodded. He was fine with Talmirov's absence, although he wasn't exactly thrilled about hanging out with all of the dictator's buddies either. He hoped this would be a short event.

After they went down the stairs and passed the front desk, Jaxon noticed an unusually large number of men slouching in the lobby with cigarettes and suspicious stares. Military types with guns flanked the front door. Halyna guided them instead through a set of double doors, down a short corridor, and into a room resembling every hotel meeting space on the planet: moveable walls, ugly carpet, and chandeliers that gave off a markedly jaundiced light. Stackable chairs surrounded a dozen cloth-draped round tables, while a long rectangular table dominated the front of the room. Almost every seat was occupied by men in suits and uniforms and their more colorfully dressed wives, and every person in the place turned to face Jaxon and his party as they entered. After a brief pause, the attendees clapped.

Jaxon executed an awkward little bow and then allowed Halyna to tow him to the long table. When they got there, Reid was consigned to the nearest round table while Jaxon was directed to a chair at the middle of the rectangle. "I prefer my assistant nearby," he said, hoping he didn't sound like a kid clinging to his parents on the first day of kindergarten.

"Do not worry," Halyna said. "Albina and I will translate for you." She waved at the spot next to Jaxon's, where Albina waited in a silver dress and smiled brightly at them.

"But my assistant—"

"It's okay," Reid interrupted, although he looked displeased. He sat down where assigned, between a portly gray-haired man and a tiny woman with an elaborate hairdo. And really, it wasn't that far from Jaxon, who'd have a clear view of Reid from his own spot. Jaxon still didn't like it.

Halyna introduced Jaxon to the other people at the table of honor, all of whom seemed to be deputy ministers of some kind, and when Jaxon sat, she took the chair on the other side of him.

"How come Mariya has to miss out on the festivities?" Jaxon asked, reaching for his glass of water.

The two guides exchanged worried glances before Albina answered. "Unfortunately, she is ill and cannot join us."

She'd seemed fine the previous day, but some things could come on quickly. Jaxon pictured her sitting at home in pajamas with a cup of her herbal tea and a good book, and he was a little envious. He'd rather be puking into a toilet than sitting in this room. "Sorry to hear that. I hope she feels better soon."

Halyna and Albina answered with smiles that seemed more nervous than sincere. Before Jaxon could figure out why, one of the deputy ministers stood and clinked a spoon against his water glass. Then he gave a long, boring speech about the wonders of Vasnytsian traditional music and dance. Next came a different guy's speech about the wonders of Vasnytsian history, then one about the wonders of Vasnytsian government, and so on. Albina and Halyna took turns whispering translations into Jaxon's ear, but he didn't pay much attention. Mostly he watched Reid, who appeared uneasy. Was he having second thoughts about their bathroom tryst?

At long last, the speeches ended and food appeared. Although the meal was bland—chicken, rolls, and some kind of cooked greens—it at least wasn't drowning in butter and cream. Jaxon ate politely and sipped at a glass of red wine, relieved to learn that he wasn't expected to make conversation. In fact, he wasn't sure why he was there at all. Maybe just as proof of Talmirov's power. After all, the prime minister had managed to drag a rock star to his isolated little country.

There was apple cake for dessert, along with more wine. And just when Jaxon was hoping the banquet might be over, more people gave speeches. Eventually Albina informed Jaxon that he was supposed to say something too. Despite the fact that he was a singer, not a public speaker, he stood and managed a few phrases of appreciation for Vasnytsian hospitality. Halyna translated, and the crowd seemed pleased. They smiled and clapped, at any rate.

Finally the informal portion of the evening arrived. While the guides kept Jaxon tethered to his chair, the guests took turns approaching him, each offering a few words. He felt like a prince receiving supplicants, and he was strongly tempted to throw ironic glances at Reid, who hovered close by.

"Your music is very interesting," announced an attractive young woman with a much older husband. She spoke English—a nice change—but was flirting openly enough to make Jaxon uncomfortable and bring a scowl to her husband's face.

Jaxon gave her a professional smile, the one he used for the hundredth person to ask him for a selfie while he was trying to take a morning run. "Thank you. I hope you enjoyed the concert."

"Oh, yes, very much." She began to rhapsodize about her favorite songs, but Jaxon just nodded whenever she paused. His main attention was still on Reid, who'd just accepted a glass of wine from a waiter. Jaxon didn't know if that was a good sign or bad; Reid had been sticking to water all night.

Fortunately, the woman's husband soon dragged her away, and Reid stepped in before anyone could take her place. "How are you holding up?" he asked Jaxon.

"Okay."

"Your throat's not sore?"

Something in Reid's tone signaled that he was offering an escape; Jaxon latched on immediately. "Actually, it kind of is. Scratchy."

Reid set his wineglass down and leaned across the table. "Let me see," he ordered.

A little weird to be playing doctor now, but Jaxon obediently opened wide. Reid peered inside. "Tsk," Reid said, shaking his head. "It's red. You need to rest it. Maybe we can get more of that tea from Mariya."

Halyna was thin-lipped. "Mariya is ill."

"Oh," said Reid. But he appeared a bit shaken. "Well anyway, Jaxon needs to rest now before he damages his vocal cords."

Although Jaxon's vocal cords were just fine, he nodded his agreement. "I do." He tried to inject a bit of hoarseness into it.

"I think perhaps guests expected Mr. Powers to sing," said Albina with a frown.

Reid shook his head. "Then they'll be disappointed. He's still recovering from the concert yesterday and can't put more stress on his throat."

"Just one song?"

"No, not even one. He's done enough with all the talking tonight."

In truth, Jaxon wouldn't have objected to a short set; it was preferable to making a speech, at least. But he was enjoying this little battle of wills, with Albina scowling furiously and Reid as implacable as a mountain. Halyna, like Jaxon, remained a spectator.

"These are very important people," Albina said.

"Jaxon Powers is also very important. I won't allow him to be injured just to entertain some dignitaries." They were arguing in English, possibly for Jaxon's benefit but more likely so that few of the bystanders would understand. But quite a few people were watching, and none of them could have mistaken Albina and Reid's body language.

At this point Jaxon could have just marched out of the room, but he was trapped between Halyna and Albina. He couldn't get out without pushing one of them aside, and that seemed excessively rude. Besides, he trusted Reid to free him soon.

Albina was clearly considering new ways to state her case. When she realized her wineglass was empty, she picked up Reid's, defiantly drank it dry, and slammed it down onto the tablecloth. "Prime Minister Talmirov will be displeased."

"Then you can send him our regrets. Tell him Jaxon is also a busy man who can't afford to be laid up. Not only does he have another concert, but when he gets back to the States, he has a record to finish."

But Albina didn't budge. With a determined expression, Reid stomped around the table and got in Albina's face. She was tall, especially in heels, but he was taller still, and broader. To her credit, she didn't back down. "Mr. Stanfill, you are being unreasonable."

"I'm doing my job."

For several moments, Reid and Albina stared each other down in silence. Then she glanced around and, noticing the audience, sighed in resignation. "Perhaps we can…." Her sentence trailed off and she held a palm to her forehead.

Reid's aggressive stance changed immediately and he took a step closer. "Albina? What's wrong?"

"I… I can't…." She muttered something in Vasnytsian and staggered back, almost crashing into Jaxon. When she reached for the table for support, she knocked over Jaxon's half-full glass, sending a small flood of bloodred wine over the cloth and onto the carpet. Jaxon and Reid both reached out to steady her, but she clutched her stomach and doubled over. Her breathing sounded harsh and rapid. With a loud gasp, she collapsed completely, landing facedown near the wall. Reid knelt and turned her over, tightening his jaw when he saw her cherry-red face.

Reid looked up at Jaxon. "I'm so sorry, Jax. But you'll be safe." Then he shot to his feet, pushed past several dignitaries, and ran out a back door.

Chapter Nine

FOR a long, shuddery moment, complete stillness filled the banquet hall. Jaxon remained frozen with Albina motionless at his feet. Then someone in uniform barked at him in Vasnytsian and pushed him aside to get to Albina. Jaxon shot a desperate look at Halyna, but her eyes were saucer-wide and both hands covered her mouth. No help from that quarter.

He swore, took a few deep breaths, and sprinted after Reid.

The exit led to a dark, narrow corridor. A right turn, Jaxon was fairly certain, would take him toward the lobby, while turning left meant heading toward an unassuming door. Guessing that Reid wanted to avoid the crowd in the lobby, Jaxon turned left. He was wearing those damn boots with heels, and Reid had a good head start. But Jaxon was still fast, and when he burst through the door and into an alley, he saw Reid just disappearing around the far corner.

Silently cursing every heavy meal he'd been forced to consume over the past few days, Jaxon pressed himself harder and picked up speed.

Three blocks later, he'd nearly caught up. But suddenly Reid spun around, a knife in one hand, the blade glittering in the moonlight.

"Reid!" Jaxon cried, skidding to a halt.

After a half beat, Reid tucked the knife away. Their heavy breathing echoed on the deserted street. "Go back!" Reid growled.

"No."

Snarling, Reid surged forward, grabbed Jaxon's arm, and dragged him into a space between two buildings, not even wide enough to be an alley. Jaxon had no idea what purpose it might have served five hundred years earlier when this part of the city was built, but now it contained tattered pieces of paper and a few plastic bags.

Reid pushed Jaxon against a stone wall and stood chest to chest, but this time no kisses ensued. "This isn't a game, Jaxon. You need to go back."

"What the fuck's going on?"

"Poison."

"What?"

Reid made an animal noise and punched the wall next to Jaxon. "Cyanide. Albina drank my wine and got the cyanide meant for me."

An image flashed into Jaxon's mind, as clear as a photo: Reid sprawled unmoving on the banquet room's ugly carpet, his chest still and his face bright red. Jaxon's stomach tightened and he clutched Reid's shoulders. "W-why was there cyanide in your wine?" The ground seemed to be tilting beneath him, and it wasn't just the recent dash that made it hard to breathe.

Then Reid shocked him further by leaning against him and resting his head on Jaxon's shoulder. "I'm sorry," Reid whispered. "Lies. Half-truths. God, I'm so sorry."

"So be honest with me now."

With a deep sigh, Reid pulled away. "I can't. Look, you're safe. You're too high profile for them to target. Go back to the hotel. Tell them you couldn't find me. Pretend you believe them when they say Albina choked to death or died of an embolism."

"But...." Jaxon shook his head hard, hoping to clear it. "I don't understand."

"Good. *Please*, Jax. Go."

"Where are you going?"

Reid rubbed his forehead. "I don't know. I need to find a way out of the country."

And then the realization hit. Belatedly, yes, but maybe the night's events excused Jaxon's slow mind. "You're a spy!"

The look he received in response held both impatience and pity. "I'm an intelligence officer."

Jaxon nodded. "Right. A spy. What are you spying on? Who's trying to kill you?" Then a thought struck him. "Jesus—who are you spying *for*?"

"I work for the US State Department, just like I told you from the start. And I don't want to put you in danger. Go back to the hotel."

"You're in danger."

Reid twitched his shoulders impatiently. "That's what I signed on for. It's my job. You're—"

"Just a guy who sings. Right."

"Fuck!" Reid looked like he wanted to punch the wall again. "That's not what I mean. You agreed to do a couple of concerts, which is great. You didn't agree to put your life on the line. And I sure as hell didn't approve of you getting involved with this end of it. Go back to the hotel."

It was funny, but the more times Reid ordered him to leave, the less Jaxon wanted to. He crossed his arms and held his ground.

"Dammit, Jax! This isn't—"

"A game. I know. You already said that." And just like that, he made a decision. "I'm going with you."

"No, you're not."

"Yes, I am. I'm going to follow you. I run faster than you, even in these heels. So unless you're planning to stab me, you're stuck with me."

This time Reid did punch the wall. His knuckles came away bloody. "Why the fuck are you doing this? Go back to the hotel and you'll be safe. You can go on with your life. Go back to your fancy suites and your pretty one-night stands and your goddamn platinum records." His voice had risen, but now he lowered it. "If you come with me, you'll almost certainly end up dead."

"I'll end up dead anyway," Jaxon replied with a small smile. "We all will, in the end. This... mission. This thing they're trying to murder you over. Is it the right thing to do? Are you wearing a white hat?"

"There are no white hats. Just varying shades of gray."

"Reid."

"I... I think I'm one of the good guys."

Jaxon nodded. "Then I'm going with you."

"You're not trained in any of this. You'll just get in my way."

Apparently Jaxon's brain, perhaps making up for its previous lapses, had jumped a few steps ahead. "No, I'll help you. You need to flee the country, right? And great, you speak the language, good for you, but why would any Vasnytsians risk prison or worse to give you a hand? Me, on the other hand—I have fans here. I bet some of them might be willing to help me out."

"Or not. You may be famous, but you're not immune. If you take active steps to support me, Talmirov won't care how many Grammys you've won. He'll take you down too."

"Could be worse," said Jaxon, who honestly wasn't afraid. "I could OD, or choke on my own vomit, or just croak from irrelevance while playing at the Box Butte County Fair. I'd rather be the only rock star in history who was assassinated while helping a spy."

"That's idiotic." But Jaxon could tell that Reid was wavering.

"I may be idiotic, but I'm also stubborn. I'm used to getting my way."

"This isn't like asking for no red M&M's backstage, Jax. It's—"

"Life-and-death. I get it. And they were brown M&M's. Plus there was a legit reason for Van Halen to put that in their contracts. It was a safety issue, actually."

Reid stared at him for a moment before rolling his eyes. "They'll be here soon. I need to get somewhere safe."

"*We* need to, yes. Do you have any ideas?"

"I think," Reid said, tugging on Jaxon's lapel, "we need to start by blending in a little better."

He'd said *we*.

Jaxon grinned.

IT was difficult to skulk through a strange city while wearing a flashy suit and high-heeled boots, but Jaxon did his best. It helped that even though it wasn't especially late, almost all the businesses were closed for the night and few locals wandered the streets. But Jaxon and Reid still had to avoid cafés where people sat at outdoor tables or inside near the windows, nursing their coffee and smoking.

"Why are they trying to kill you?" Jaxon whispered as he and Reid crept down an alley smelling of garbage. "What's your real mission?"

"I'll tell you later."

"We better not get killed before you do. I'd end up a really pissed-off ghost."

Reid ignored him.

A few blocks later, they reached the part of the city built under Austro-Hungarian rule. The structures were blocky and gray, with crumbling plaster exposing the concrete-and-wood walls beneath. The majority of the few streetlights were burned out, but the moon was almost full. As he walked down the sidewalks, sticking close to the walls, Reid seemed to be searching for something. Almost all the buildings had large courtyards in the center, most of them blocked by wooden or chain-link gates. But Reid found one of the wooden gates ajar, and he and Jaxon slipped inside.

Lights from the surrounding windows illuminated the courtyard, revealing cracked pavement littered with crumpled paper and broken bits of plastic and metal— the remains of toys and machines. But several large pots were growing vegetables, and laundry hung on long rope lines. Reid spent some time inspecting the hanging clothes before selecting a plain yellow polo shirt and a pair of gray tracksuit pants. He brought them over and handed them to Jaxon. "Put these on," he ordered quietly.

Although the clothing wasn't exactly Jaxon's style, he didn't argue, and the stolen clothes fit well. He felt bad for whomever they belonged to and hoped his Grammy suit, abandoned in the courtyard, would compensate for the loss.

But Reid wasn't satisfied. "Those damn boots," he said, staring at Jaxon's feet.

"I don't think anyone has shoes hanging on a clothesline."

"No." Reid ditched his jacket and tie. In plain slacks and a white button-down, he'd blend in reasonably well with the locals.

"How come I don't hear sirens?" Jaxon asked as they made their way back to the street. "Aren't they after us?"

"Yes, but they'll want to keep it low-key, at least for now. And they'll be confident we won't get far."

"Are they right about that?"

Reid looked grim. "I don't know."

Not reassuring. Yet Jaxon followed him in spite of having no clue where they were heading. If it hadn't been for glimpses of the hill with the ruined castle, he would have been completely lost. After about twenty minutes, they arrived in a somewhat affluent neighborhood—by Vasnytsian standards—at the base of the hill. Two- and three-story houses squatted among apartment buildings, all in reasonably good condition, and modest shops lined a few of the streets. Reid paused in front of a window that displayed men's shoes and clothing.

Jaxon realized what was going on. "Oh no, you're not—"

"Shh!" After a quick look around, Reid took them down an alley to the back of the building. He stopped at a door, took an object from his pocket, and did something to the lock. Jaxon couldn't see the details in the dark, but within seconds the lock opened with a quiet click and Reid opened the door.

"What if there's an alarm?" Jaxon whispered.

"Isn't. No alarms here."

Reid closed the door as soon as they were inside. While he ventured deeper into the store, Jaxon remained near the wall, having a flashback to when he was eight and stole a package of gum from Neth's Pharmacy. His mother had discovered the wrappers in his bedroom and had marched him to Neth's to confess and apologize, and his father had yelled at him and grounded him for a month. He suspected the consequences of being caught burglarizing this shop would be rather more dire.

It didn't take long for Reid to find a cheap pair of running shoes and a lightweight jacket to fit Jaxon. They threw his boots into a garbage bin a few blocks away. "Now where?" Jaxon asked.

"Quiet. I'm thinking." But judging from his expression, Reid was fresh out of ideas. He kept rubbing his forehead.

As they turned a corner, a small cat dashed in front of them, squeezed through a tiny window at sidewalk level, and disappeared into a basement. Jaxon stopped in his tracks. "The Black Cat."

Reid waved distractedly at him. "It was white."

"With black spots. But I wasn't talking about the actual cat."

"I'm trying to save our asses here. Could you just—"

"Remember when we went to the potato kitchen?"

"Yes." Reid scowled at him.

"A guy told me about this place called the Black Cat, where—"

"What guy?"

Before Jaxon could answer, loud male voices sounded from somewhere close by. They might have been just drunks heading home from a bar, but maybe not. Reid took off running with Jaxon at his side. They ducked into the next open courtyard gate they came to and huddled under the building's archway.

Reid picked up the conversation where he'd dropped it. "What guy?"

"One of the other customers. We exchanged a few words when I stopped to tie my shoe."

"Jesus, Jax. He could've gone to prison for that."

"He spoke with me first," said Jaxon, who didn't appreciate being scolded like a child. "And he said he and his friends listen to my music all the time at a place called the Black Cat. Maybe someone there…?"

Reid was staring at him. "Cherna Koshka."

"What?"

"It means black cat. Mariya mentioned it to me. She said the people there were sympathetic."

"To what?"

"Us," Reid said grimly.

"So let's go there!"

"Sure, great, except I don't know where the hell it is." After a moment of forehead rubbing, Reid acquired a determined expression. "Okay. Come with me."

It seemed logical to ask where they were going if Reid didn't know how to find the Black Cat, but Jaxon kept his mouth shut, figuring he'd find out eventually. By the time they'd walked over a mile and had begun to climb the hill, he was regretting his discretion. "No way the Black Cat's in Talmirov's backyard."

"That's not where we're going. Hurry up."

They didn't quite run, but they went at a good clip, keeping to the heavy greenery at the side of the road.

Twice they heard cars coming uphill; both times they ducked into the bushes and the cars passed without incident. Almost an hour later, they reached the top of the hill, where the abandoned castle ruins sprawled in the moonlight.

"Why?" asked Jaxon, looking around in bewilderment.

"It's late and things are going to be really hot for a few hours. We're going to hide out here until morning, when I hope the authorities will have cooled a little, and then I'll try to track down Cherna Koshka."

It made rough sense, and Jaxon certainly didn't have a better plan, so he trailed Reid into the thick woods beside the ruins. In most of the United States, those woods would have been littered with beer cans, used condoms, and maybe hypodermic needles, but here they seemed pristine—at least as far as he could tell in the dark.

At the bottom of a tiny valley, under the thick cover of tree boughs, Reid stopped and collapsed elegantly onto the ground, where he sat with his knees bent. For the first time, Jaxon sensed something like despair coming from him

"What's wrong?" Jaxon asked as he sat close beside him.

"What's wrong? Albina's dead. Mariya's possibly dead too, or at least in prison. I have no idea how the hell I'm going to get out of this mess. And I've managed to drag you into it. You were just my ticket to Vasnytsia. You were supposed to stay safe."

"Safe is overrated."

Reid simply grunted.

After several minutes, Jaxon leaned against him. "Will you explain now what's going on? What's our secret mission?"

"It's *my* mission. You're—"

"The ticket. Yeah, yeah. Why did you need a ticket?"

Without answering, Reid unbuttoned and removed his shirt, keeping his undershirt on. "I needed this," he said, patting his left bicep.

"A bandage?"

"Mariya injected me with a microchip."

"So the dogcatcher can find your owners if you get lost?"

"What? No! Jax, this is—"

"Not a game." Jaxon sighed. "Don't you have a sense of humor at all?"

"Not when lives are at stake."

Jaxon shrugged. It seemed to him that a bit of levity was especially useful in a crisis. But he didn't say so. "So there's a chip?" he prompted.

"It contains classified documents. Some of them implicate Talmirov in corruption. We've known for years that he's been stealing from the government and stashing the money overseas, but this is the proof we needed."

Jaxon thought about that for a few moments. "So if those documents get into the right hands...."

"Talmirov's opponents here would probably find enough support to feel comfortable turning on him. There would be a coup—a peaceful one, if we're lucky."

"What if the opponents are assholes too?"

"We—the intelligence community, I mean—have been vetting them. We're prepared to provide assistance to the right ones."

Under other circumstances, Jaxon would have been critical of the United States attempting to influence a foreign government. It didn't seem right—and similar policies had turned out disastrously elsewhere. But he'd seen the kind of life Vasnytsians had to endure, and he knew they'd been stuck that way for decades. Maybe some intervention wasn't a bad thing.

"So you're carrying the info that could bring Talmirov down," Jaxon said.

"Yes, but there's more. Possibly even more important documents. I don't even know all the details on this part, just the bare bones. Moscow apparently has its eyes on more than just Crimea. There are several other former Soviet territories they'd like to bring back into the fold. Talmirov's apparently agreed to give the Russians a cozy western base of operations for some of these efforts."

"In exchange for more zillions for his overseas bank accounts?"

"Bingo." Reid turned to face him, although he couldn't have seen well. "Explain to me why someone who's already incredibly wealthy would be so eager for more. Do the millions lose their meaning after a while?"

"Yes," Jaxon answered immediately. He wasn't evil-dictator rich, but he had plenty. And he remembered how ecstatic he'd been when, not too long out of Nebraska, he got a gig that paid a couple of thousand a month. Nowadays he'd drop several grand without even thinking about it. Hell, those boots now sitting in a Starograd garbage can had cost over three thousand dollars. And he'd just casually thrown them away.

"What happens if people find out what Talmirov and the Russians have been up to?" Jaxon asked.

"At the very least, sanctions against Russia. But quite likely more. The international stage is a complicated place right now, and anything Russia does casts wide ripples."

Ignoring the mixed metaphor, Jaxon nodded. "Okay. So you need to get that chip into the right hands." But then another thought struck him. "Why was Mariya involved with the chip?"

"She's—well she *was*—one of our assets. She had access to all sorts of information, mostly through her father. Deputy minister of defense."

Right. She'd mentioned something about that. "But she's not a Talmirov fan?"

"No. A lot of people here are against him. But it's terribly risky to speak out."

That reminded Jaxon that Reid had come very close to dying earlier that night. Shuddering, he draped an arm around Reid's shoulders, as if that would keep him safe.

"Cold?" asked Reid.

"Yes," Jaxon lied.

They sat like that for a long time, Jaxon imagining the weight of responsibility that rested on Reid's broad shoulders. Nobody had ever counted on Jaxon like that. If he fucked up a song, nobody died. Countries wouldn't rise or fall because of it.

After a while and still without speaking, Jaxon and Reid lay down on the ground, which was soft with shed pine needles. They huddled close together for comfort and warmth and listened to the small night sounds.

"Not quite a five-star hotel." Reid sounded sleepy.

"Reminds me of camping when I was a kid."

"Boy Scouts?"

"Nah. Parents. We'd go to Big Mac—Lake McConaughy—or up into the Black Hills and spend a week living in a tent and driving one another crazy. S'mores. Fishing. Swimming. Mosquitoes." He yawned hugely. "We used to sing together around the campfire. Totally hokey."

"It sounds like fun."

Those getaways were among his happiest childhood memories, the rare times when his parents had relaxed and they'd all enjoyed one another's company. "How about you? Did you camp when you were a kid?"

Reid didn't reply for several moments, and when he did, he sounded faraway. "No. First time I ever slept outside was in the Army." He shifted slightly in Jaxon's arms. "We need to sleep now. I'd really like to keep you alive tomorrow."

Jaxon drifted off to the sound of Reid's steady breaths.

Chapter Ten

SLEEPING on the ground was a lot easier on a ten-year-old body than one in its late thirties. Jaxon woke up sore and disoriented, with pine needles in his hair and, most likely, bugs in his clothes. He'd been missing his guitar, but now he missed his toothbrush even more.

Reid sat next to him, watching.

"What?" Jaxon demanded as he sat up and stretched.

"You sing in your sleep."

"I do not!"

"You do. Just a few words here and there. Sometimes you hum."

That was too weird to contemplate. Jaxon looked around and saw nothing but the sun's morning rays sneaking through the branches, creating designs on the ground. "I guess we're lucky the weather's good."

Still seated, Reid looked at him gravely. "You can still go back. Tell them you were scared and ran after me, and I kidnapped you."

Jaxon snorted his dismissal of the idea. "Does the State Department know we're missing?"

"I don't know. Mariya wasn't our only asset, but getting information out of the country is dangerous and difficult." He shook his head. "Doesn't matter anyway. They can't get anyone in here to extract me. Us."

"So we go to the Black Cat...."

"And hope like hell your fans are dedicated enough to hide us while I find a way out."

Thinking of some of the things people had sent him over the years, Jaxon grinned. Engagement rings. Lots and lots of fan art. Piles of underwear. And thousands of letters and emails expressing undying devotion. Buzz kept the more disturbing stuff away from him, but Jaxon still had a decent idea of how deep some people's adoration could go.

Comforted as he was by his supportive fans, another notion unsettled him. "If those people help us, they could get in deep trouble. Or dead." He shuddered as he remembered Albina's dying gasps.

"Yes," Reid said.

Yet if Jaxon and Reid didn't ask for help, their prospects were dim. Not to mention the fact that Talmirov's corruption would continue unchecked, and Russia would have help invading places, and.... Shit. Musicians rarely had to make life-and-death decisions.

"Let's go find that cat," Jaxon said.

Reid stood and brushed debris from his clothes. Even after sleeping on the ground, he looked tidy. Maybe the State Department issued special dirt- and wrinkle-proof clothing to its operatives.

"You stay here," he said.

"No! I'm coming—"

"Do you really think it's such a great idea for you to walk the streets of Starograd? People will recognize you."

Oh. Yeah. If Jaxon couldn't manage anonymity while jogging through the wonderful diversity of San Francisco, he probably couldn't pull it off while wandering here. "Can you blend in with the locals?"

"Better than you. Stay here. I'll find out where Cherna Koshka is and come back, and we'll both go there tonight."

The plan made sense, but that didn't mean Jaxon was happy about it. "What am I supposed to do here?"

"Nothing. Lay low. You should be able to hear if anyone approaches, in which case head in the other direction and hide. The woods are surprisingly thick up here. Just don't get lost—I need to find you when I return."

"What if you don't return?" Jaxon asked it quietly, hoping he sounded calm.

Reid worked his jaw. "If I don't come back, it's because I can't. I won't willingly abandon you. If... if they catch me, I'm going to confess to forcing you to run away with me. So if I'm not back by tonight, head back to the hotel."

Jaxon was going to protest, but Reid stopped him with a raised hand. "Don't be stupid, Jax. It'll be your best chance of surviving. If you get caught trying to escape on your own—and you *will* get caught—it's not going to help anyone."

All Jaxon could do was nod.

Then suddenly Reid had his arms around Jaxon, holding him tight, his lips a whisper away from Jaxon's ear. "You are an interesting man," Reid said before kissing him with a desperate hunger Jaxon had only imagined before.

Jaxon was just as ravenous, and for a few moments he forgot about spies and cyanide and dictators and microchips. For a too-brief pulse of time, it was just Reid and him under the trees, their passion as weighty as the earth beneath them.

Reid pulled slightly away and traced a thumb across Jaxon's lip. "I will come back for you if I can."

Jaxon believed him.

THE hours passed slowly. Jaxon's stomach burned from hunger and anxiety, his mouth was parched, and despite his worry, he was totally and profoundly bored. For someone who'd been craving isolation, the reality proved a disappointment. He was used to conversation around him, to a world full of amusements at his fingertips. Now he didn't even have a phone to play games on; he'd left it in his hotel room before the banquet.

He desperately wanted his guitar.

He ended up sitting on the soft ground, listening to the music of the forest—tree branches whispering, insects rustling among leaves, birds calling to one another. It was a sort of symphony, really, and he was the only audience. Eventually a new tune wound its way through his brain, a tune inspired by what he heard around him, and he made up some lyrics that seemed to fit. He had no way to write anything down, so he hoped he'd remember it later. Assuming he ever got his hands on a guitar again and didn't spend the rest of his life in a Vasnytsian prison. Or end up drinking cyanide for dinner.

Then he thought about Reid and the satisfying solidity of Reid asleep in his arms. Jaxon had fucked a lot of people, but he'd slept with very few.

"Now I know what a Bond girl feels like," Jaxon said—out loud, but very quietly. "If we survive this, will they make a movie of it? And if so, will I play myself?" Although he'd always considered his acting skills too weak for that kind of career expansion, maybe playing himself wouldn't be too big a stretch.

He was mentally casting the rest of the film—would Joe Manganiello make a good Reid?—when he heard footsteps coming from the direction of the castle. Before he could scurry away, a familiar voice called out in English, "Don't run. It's me."

A moment later Reid appeared over the top of the little hill. He'd somehow managed to change into a blue-and-yellow tracksuit with a gray tee, and he carried a plastic bag.

"Please tell me that's food and drink," said Jaxon, smiling up at him.

Reid grinned and nodded.

They sat cross-legged facing each other, munching on the phyllo-and-meat sandwiches that were the Starograd equivalent of hamburgers. They tasted pretty good. Reid had brought bottles of water and some liquid yogurt stuff you were supposed to drink like milk, along with a couple of apples.

"A nice picnic," Jaxon said. "Thanks. But did you find the cat?"

"Yes. It's in the old city."

"Did you have any problems?"

"No. I saw more police than usual, but I kept my head down. I don't think they recognized me."

Jaxon took a swig of yogurt. "Thank you. For coming back for me."

"I'm not...." Reid glanced away for a moment. "You're getting under my skin, and that's dangerous. I can't afford to... to care about anything but the mission."

With his heart twisting, Jaxon shook his head. "You think you're the only guy in the world with intimacy issues? I've never dated anyone for longer than a week. Ever. And yeah, maybe nobody's trying to poison me, but that doesn't mean I don't hurt." Ha. His therapist would be very proud—if Jaxon hadn't given up on seeing him years ago.

"I was married," said Reid. "Right after high school. My stab at living a normal life. Poor girl."

"Oh my God—did someone assassinate her?" Jaxon pictured a young woman lying motionless on a suburban living room floor.

Reid rolled his eyes. "We divorced less than a year later. The whole 'normal' thing wasn't working out. That's when I enlisted." He wadded up his empty food wrapper and stuffed it into the bag. "I haven't talked to her since. I hope things went well for her."

Reid's confession didn't especially shock Jaxon, but one aspect of it caught his attention. "You didn't have a normal life when you were a kid?"

"No interrogations," Reid replied as he collected the rest of the trash. "My childhood doesn't matter, and talking about it would just make the under-the-skin thing worse."

"Fine. But if we get out of here, you owe me a biography. You had some kind of dossier on me, and I've got nothing on you. It's not fair."

"If we get out of here, I'm going to spend about a million years in debriefing. I'll also be skinned alive for allowing their cherished rock star to get involved."

Jaxon clenched his jaw to keep from starting a fight. He didn't have the energy for it, not right now. And seemingly neither did Reid, who yawned and stretched. "We have time before dark, and I didn't sleep much last night. Would you keep watch while I catch a few winks?"

That small show of trust mollified Jaxon a little. "Okay." Somehow he ended up with Reid's head in his lap, which was unexpectedly pleasant. Jaxon stroked Reid's soft crew cut and hummed quietly until Reid's body relaxed and his breathing slowed.

Asleep, he didn't look like a model or a spy— he was just an exhausted man with a day's growth of whiskers and phyllo crumbs on his jacket.

"You're already under my skin," Jaxon said. But unless the woods were bugged, nobody heard him.

CLOUDS had moved in by early evening, obscuring the moon and darkening the woods. Reid seemed to have little difficulty finding his way to the castle ruins, and Jaxon stuck close behind him. As they crept down the hill, traffic seemed heavier than before, with big, dark vehicles entering and leaving the prime minister's palace. It took Reid and Jaxon a long time to descend because they were repeatedly forced to hide in the bushes.

Once they reached the flat part of the city, they moved more swiftly. Some people were out and about—mostly factory workers on their way home— but Jaxon kept his head down and mouth shut, and nobody seemed to recognize him. It helped that the streets were dark and that the cheap tracksuits allowed Jaxon and Reid to blend in with the locals.

They passed quite a few uniformed men with guns, most of whom looked utterly bored and were too busy smoking to pay much attention. It appeared that state security wasn't a top priority for much of the rank and file. But when Jaxon and Reid turned a corner near the old city, they were just in time to see a squad of soldiers turn onto the same street a block away—heading toward them. And these guys looked like they meant business. They marched in step, guns slung over their shoulders, faces set in stern masks. Jaxon's heart beat a fast rhythm as he realized these men were coming after him.

But it turned out that maybe his acting skills weren't so awful after all, because he feigned nonchalance and continued onward, Reid several steps ahead. They weren't a fugitive intelligence officer and a rock star— they were nothing but tired Vasnytsians coming home from work, or maybe heading to a café or bar for a drink. In the low light, Jaxon's hallmark red hair simply appeared dark and unremarkable.

Jaxon breathed a noisy sigh of relief after the soldiers marched past without glancing his way, and his heart attempted to reach a healthier speed.

Secrecy became easier in the old city, where the streets were narrower and more deeply shadowed and where alleys and odd nooks provided easy hiding spaces. But there were also more people here, many of them sitting on front steps or clustered around outdoor tables. They smoked and chatted quietly, and Jaxon was suddenly struck by the complete absence of music. Not a single open door spilled notes out onto the street. This particular silence, perhaps more than anything, made Jaxon understand how difficult life was for Vasnytsians.

Reid entered a small café that had five or six occupied tables out front, and Jaxon followed him closely. Jaxon hadn't been able to read the sign, but he didn't really need to since it featured a black cat arching its back. Only a few of the inside tables were taken, probably because the warm evening made sitting outside more attractive. Reid chose a small table near the back.

The café was largely unremarkable—stone walls adorned with the requisite Talmirov posters, a well-worn floor, and a wood-beamed ceiling. The air was thick with cigarette smoke. Two young waiters ferried trays of coffee to the customers, and an older woman worked behind the glass-and-wood counter, preparing drinks and washing dishes.

Reid didn't have to say what an enormous risk they were taking. Even if Jaxon hadn't been fully aware of their situation, the stiffness of Reid's shoulders and the tightness of his jaw would have transmitted the sense of danger. As for Jaxon, he felt slightly nauseous. And since he had no clue how to proceed, he decided the best course of action was keeping his lips zipped.

After a few minutes, one of the waiters approached. Reid ordered coffees for both of them—Jaxon caught that much of the conversation—and his accent must have been good, because the waiter simply nodded and left. That gave Jaxon time to consider the things that might happen next; few of them were good. It disturbed him that the guy in the potato kitchen had claimed to listen to Jaxon's music every night here— yet nobody was listening to any music at all. Christ, if Jaxon had misled Reid, then Reid's capture, his possible death, and the fates of Vasnytsia and assorted former Soviet republics would all be Jaxon's doing. He hoped Talmirov would have him shot quickly, before he endured too much torture by his own conscience.

The waiter appeared with their coffees and Reid gave him a few coins. How had he gotten his hands on Vasnytsian money? Their guides had paid for the few expenses outside the hotel. As Jaxon tried to puzzle that through, someone across the room gave a loud laugh, a rare sound in Starograd. Jaxon turned to look, and it was nothing more than some coveralled men and women playing cards. But they caught Jaxon looking, and their widening eyes let him know that they recognized him.

A man at a nearby table stood up and started over. Just as Jaxon was ready to shout at Reid to make a run for it, he recognized the man—the guy from the potato kitchen. "Jaxon Powers!" he whispered when he was close. "Where is guide?"

Jaxon glanced at Reid, who gave him a go-ahead gesture. "No guide," Jaxon said quietly. "But we really need your help. Please."

"What help?"

"Talmirov's after us."

Their potential savior was an ordinary-looking fellow dressed in gray-blue coveralls frayed around the collar and cuffs. He was tall and skinny, with poorly cut brown hair, teeth in need of straightening, and whiskers a couple of days old. But as he stood staring at Jaxon, the man's eyes shone and his mouth stretched into a wide smile. This was a person discovering he could be a hero—and he transformed from ordinary to beautiful.

"Wait," the man ordered before rushing to the counter. During the quiet but intense conversation, the barista stared at Jaxon and Reid, her face expressionless. But at the end she nodded, which seemed to please Jaxon's new friend.

"Come," said the man as soon as he returned to the table. Moving quickly, Reid and Jaxon followed him through a door near the counter and down a flight of ancient, narrow stairs. At the bottom was a single bathroom and a large storage closet. Jaxon was somewhat alarmed when they were led into the closet, weakly lit by a single bare light bulb, but Reid seemed willing to go, so Jaxon followed. The man shut the door, cramming the three of them between wooden shelves stacked with waiters' aprons, napkins, dishes, and cleaning supplies. The man performed a complicated knock on one of the shelves—a pattern Jaxon recognized immediately as the chorus of the Rolling Stones' "Sympathy for the Devil." To Jaxon's astonishment, the entire shelving unit swung forward, revealing a doorway.

Without a moment's hesitation, Reid stepped inside.

Chapter Eleven

AS secret rooms went, it wasn't particularly exciting. It was a large space, probably spanning many of the storefronts above, with dusty beams and several large pillars. The floor and walls were stone, worn from centuries of use, and the few hanging light bulbs cast pools of brightness surrounded by shadows. The room smelled of beer and damp, and the air was chilly enough to make Jaxon shiver in his thin jacket.

But the White Stripes played from a couple of speakers, and two dozen people in their twenties lounged on battered couches and threadbare armchairs. It was a more casual gathering than Jaxon had seen in Vasnytsia—or it had been casual, until Jaxon and Reid entered the room.

Jaxon's friend from the potato kitchen addressed the group in rapid-fire Vasnytsian. Jaxon couldn't understand anything but his own name, but Reid listened closely. By the time the little speech ended, everyone was gaping. Then an awkward, expectant hush fell, and Jaxon realized they were waiting for him to say something.

"Reid?" Jaxon asked.

"Better for them to hear it from you. I'll translate."

"Okay." After a deep breath in and out, Jaxon waved at his audience. "Uh, hi. I'm Jaxon Powers. Obviously. I was invited here for a couple of concerts." He paused so Reid could repeat his words in Vasnytsian. Jaxon got the sense that most of these people understood at least some English, but it was best that they hear the tale in their native language. He didn't want misunderstandings.

"This is Reid. He's, uh…."

Reid nodded. "You can tell them. We need to be honest now."

"Okay. He's pretending to be my assistant, but he's actually a spy. I mean, intelligence agent."

Their audience gasped, and Jaxon didn't blame them. Surely none of this was what they'd expected tonight.

"So Reid has some info that's pretty damaging to your prime minister. But it looks like Talmirov figured that out, and he tried to kill Reid. Now we're on the lam." Was there a Vasnytsian equivalent of that phrase? Apparently, because Reid said something that made everyone look even more shocked.

"We need to get out of Vasnytsia," Jaxon continued, "but we don't have any way to do that. When we visited a potato kitchen, I met, uh…." He blushed slightly. "Sorry. I don't know your name."

But the man didn't seem upset. "I am Fedir." He even gave a small bow.

"I met Fedir, and he told me he enjoys my music, that you guys listen to it here at the Black Cat. I understand that sharing this with me was a dangerous thing for him to do. Fedir's a brave man, and I am so honored."

It was Fedir's turn to blush. Jaxon was afraid Fedir's friends might be angry at him for divulging the existence of their secret little club, but they didn't seem upset. In fact, a couple of them called out what seemed to be congratulatory phrases, and a woman with an elfin face and frizzy hair ran over to kiss Fedir's cheek.

When the fuss died down, Jaxon faced the crowd. "This is asking a lot of you. I know this. But it's important. Can you help us?"

Reid hadn't even finished translating when everyone surged forward to pat Jaxon's shoulder and shake his hand. "We will help," said Fedir, who seemed to have appointed himself spokesman. "Maybe we all die. But we have, um, motto here." He said something in Vasnytsian.

With a grim smile, Reid translated, "Better a worthy death than an unworthy life."

"It sounds like something a Klingon would say."

Reid rolled his eyes.

THE actual scheming was best done in Vasnytsian, which was all right with Jaxon since he had little to contribute anyway. While Reid got deep into conversation with several people, Jaxon drank a beer and ate another of those phyllo sandwiches, both brought to him by Fedir.

"So you guys hang out here and listen to music?" Jaxon asked.

Fedir nodded eagerly. "Yes. It is one place like this. There are others in city. We talk too. Say forbidden things. Think forbidden thoughts. We taste freedom." He shrugged. "Only small taste. We dream of…. Our government, it is like metal fist—hard and strong. We dream of open hand instead." He held his own palm up to demonstrate.

"Do other people agree with you?"

"Yes, very many. But we are afraid to *do*. Maybe there are more of us, but they have guns. We have only ourselves."

Jaxon couldn't imagine such powerlessness. Even as a lonely, weird kid in Nebraska, he'd always hoped for something better. That hope had given him the courage to leave everything behind and try life on his own. What would it be like to have to endure without the option of escape?

"How do you even know about me? I thought you guys were pretty isolated from outside influences."

Fedir looked thoughtful as he toyed with some frayed threads at his knee. "It is… hard. But some people know how to make… make ways to do things. I fix machines in factory where gun is made. But also I know how to fix other machines. Other people, they do computers at work. Maybe they do computers after work also. We have… how you say? Equipment?" He removed a flip phone from a pocket and waved it a bit. "Sometimes we make it do more than government knows." He looked at Jaxon, clearly hoping for understanding.

"I get it. Job skills come in handy for other things too, and technology can be altered. But—and I realize this is a weird question—why waste your time and effort on stupid stuff like my music? Especially when it's dangerous."

But Fedir was shaking his head. "No, no. Is not stupid. Things from outside—music, films, stories—they give us what we cannot get here. Like a man who eats nothing but these." He pointed at Jaxon's half-eaten phyllo sandwich. "He will live, but without joy. If he gets also even little tastes of cake or fruit sometimes, his life will be better."

Jaxon understood what Fedir meant. When he had been a miserable teenager, music had been his salvation—the thing that got him through years of loneliness and angst. "I'm really glad I've been able to do that for you. I always was fruity."

Fedir clearly didn't get the pun, which was maybe just as well. He nodded earnestly instead. "You do more. When you are born here and live here, you think maybe this is normal. No freedom? Normal. No money? Normal. Government tells you what to do? Normal. Government punishes everyone who speaks out? Normal. Your music, the other things we get from outside, they show us, remind us, this is *not* normal. That is very important. Otherwise we stop trying to fight."

Shit. Jaxon didn't have a reasonable answer to that. It wasn't as if he'd ever intended to help inspire a revolution. He hadn't even known any of this was going on. Hell, a few weeks ago, he couldn't have found Vasnytsia on a map.

He opened his mouth to say something—he didn't know what—but then the lights went out, leaving the room completely dark.

While Jaxon remained frozen, expecting somebody to start shooting, a few cigarette lighters flickered and he heard a lot of people scrambling around. Somebody moved right in front of him, and Jaxon balled his hands into fists, ready for his first physical altercation since eighth grade. But an engine roared to life, making him jump, the lights flickered back on, and he saw who was crouched in front of him: Reid, who had his back to Jaxon and had knives in both hands.

"We are safe!" Fedir told Reid. He followed with a rapid flow of Vasnytsian that made Reid relax and tuck away his blades.

Reid turned to Jaxon. "Power outage. They get them often. They have a generator."

Jaxon's fear evaporated when he saw that no soldiers had invaded the basement. Now he stared at Reid in wonder. "That was a hell of a ninja move just now."

"I have training."

"Obviously. But you were trying to protect *me*."

"Is that a problem?" Reid was looking at him as if Jaxon might be losing his marbles.

"You're the one with the top-secret info, not me. You're the one with the mission."

"Looks like now you're part of the mission too."

That made Jaxon ridiculously happy, but not so much that he lost touch with reality. "If it comes down to me or the info, though…."

Reid looked away for a moment. "I *have* to get these files out, Jax. If I don't—"

"No, I got it. I'm even okay with it. That's what I'm trying to tell you. I understand."

Reid lifted his hand and reached for Jaxon's face, but then let his arm drop. "Okay. I need to…." He gestured toward the edge of the room, where he'd been scheming.

"Sure. Hey, Reid? Can't you just email the files to someone? You guys have some internet, right?" Jaxon looked to Fedir for confirmation.

But Reid answered before Fedir could. "They do. It's spotty and unreliable—like trying to use a dial-up modem on bad phone lines, twenty years ago. I'd give it a try anyway, but I don't have any way to extract the files from the chip. The guy who made the chip and the device that encoded it got picked up by the police a couple of months ago. We're really lucky they didn't get the chip itself."

"So the only way to get the information out—"

"Is to physically get the chip across the border. Ideally you and me along with it."

Reid returned to his corner, leaving Jaxon alone with Fedir, who was scrutinizing him. "Is he your lover?" Fedir asked bluntly.

"Uh…." Jaxon was unsure how to answer. Not just because he didn't know how well a gay relationship would go over, but also because *lover* wasn't the right word for it. He didn't think a right word existed. "You knew I'm queer, right? I mean, if you've heard anything at all about me, it's hardly news."

"My mother and father love each other very much. How you and Reid talk—it is like my mother and father. Like love." After that enigmatic observation, Fedir stood. "One minute, please." He walked away, exiting through a narrow door tucked away in the shadows.

Jaxon watched as Reid, two men, and a woman bent over some papers. Occasionally one of them would write something. None of them looked happy. Jaxon should have been worried about how the escape plans were going, because that was the important thing right now. But he kept coming back to Fedir's comment about love. It was ridiculous. A cultural misunderstanding, most likely.

Still, that one little word hung there like a dirigible on fire. *Love.*

With enormous relief, Jaxon saw Fedir returning, a battered acoustic guitar in his hand. He held out the instrument as he drew close. "Maybe… if is not too much trouble…?"

"I'd love to." The least he could do was play these people a few songs.

Across the room, a woman turned off the CD player. Everyone but Reid and his little group hurried over to sit or stand near Jaxon. Their eyes shone with excitement; their mouths stretched into enormous smiles.

Jaxon preferred to play for these people, in their coveralls and cheap dresses and T-shirts, than for all the beribboned dignitaries in Vasnytsia. No stage, no sound system, no computer-controlled lights, but it was the best concert he could imagine.

He chose his most popular songs but played them more slowly, almost like ballads. It seemed fitting for this intimate audience. When he got to "Next Train," a song about a person who had always wanted to leave his small town but never worked up the courage, a woman hesitantly began singing with him. She had a nice voice. Jaxon encouraged her with a smile and a nod, and soon the whole gang was engaged in a singalong. Jaxon wanted to laugh and cry at the same time, but he just kept on playing. Afterward he shared his newest song—the one he'd written in the hotel room—about a man whose job sent him from place to place, stranding him in hotels, keeping him a stranger.

At some point Reid and the other planners joined everyone else. He stood at the back of the crowd, and although he didn't sing, his gaze never left Jaxon.

The past twenty-four hours had been fraught, and although Jaxon would have liked to continue his impromptu performance, he grew tired. Just when he was trying to think of a graceful way to end, Reid stepped forward and made an announcement in Vasnytsian. "I told them we need to sleep," he said to Jaxon.

And evidently that was going to happen right there in the basement. The couches would be an improvement over the ground, and a toilet and sink were tucked into a tiny corner closet. Someone brought them clean T-shirts, razors, and a few other toiletries.

"Door locks here," Fedir said, pointing to a sliding bolt on the inside. "Do not open unless you hear special knock."

"Sympathy for the Devil," Jaxon said with a grin.

"Yes."

A round of handshakes followed, which included thank-yous in two languages. Then Jaxon and Reid were alone. They took turns washing up in the tiny bathroom; then Jaxon collapsed onto a couch while Reid doused all of the lights except one. He chose a couch set at right angles to Jaxon's.

"We could probably both fit here, if we squished." Jaxon patted a cushion. "I don't mind squishing."

"We need to sleep, not squish."

Although Jaxon had expected that response, he was still a bit disappointed. "Do you have a plan?" he asked quietly.

Reid took so long to answer that Jaxon thought he'd fallen asleep. But then he spoke. "You won't like it."

"I don't like any of this."

"No five-star hotels. No line of groupies eager to get into your bed."

"That's not what I meant!" Jaxon wished it wasn't too dark for Reid to see his glare. "Don't be such an asshole."

"Sorry," Reid said with a rough grunt. "Look, there's no way around it—you're a liability. Not on purpose, but because people recognize you."

That was true enough, although Jaxon didn't say so. He just waited for the axe to drop.

"Talmirov's people probably put my photo out to the military by now, so they'll be looking for me, but ordinary citizens won't. They won't even know to keep an eye out, because Talmirov's sure as hell not going to advertise what's going on. So I'm a little safer without you than with."

"Yeah, I get it." Jaxon didn't like where this was going.

"The woman I was talking to tonight—Lera— drives a truck. She delivers farm implements to towns all over the country. Tomorrow she's going to get me as close to the border as she can, and I'm going to try to sneak across. We'll head north—my intel said that's the least heavily guarded place. It's fairly rough terrain."

"And me?"

"You stay put. You'll be safe here, at least for a while. If I get through, I'll ask our government to work through diplomatic channels to extract you. If I don't make it, the people we met tonight will find a way to sneak you out. Somehow."

That was a lot more ifs and maybes than Jaxon was comfortable with. Worse, though, was the idea of being separated from Reid. Not only did Jaxon feel safe with Reid at his side, but he also had the irrational feeling that Reid was safer with him. "What if we never see each other again?"

"That's… likely. Told you from the start—this is a shitstorm. I'm just trying to dig out as fast as I can." After a moment Reid sighed. "But if we both make it, I promise we *will* see each other. You can get me a ticket to your next concert."

"Fuck that. I don't want to *sing* to you, Reid."

In a smaller voice than Jaxon would have thought possible, Reid said, "I like it when you sing." He shifted on his couch, making the springs protest. And then suddenly he was on Jaxon's couch—on Jaxon. Chest to chest and belly to belly, his breath smelling of herbal Vasnytsian toothpaste and his fingers threaded through Jaxon's hair. "You drive me crazy," he whispered.

"I-want-to-jump-your-bones crazy? I'm-going-to-strangle-you crazy? I-need-my-Xanax crazy?"

"Yes. All of the above."

Jaxon, who usually hated to be tied down by anything, loved the weight of Reid atop him. He loved feeling Reid's heartbeat and hearing his breaths. He loved tracing Reid's square jawline with a fingertip. "What are you going to do about that, Agent Stanfill?"

"Don't have any Xanax. These people won't help me if I strangle you. Guess that leaves me just one choice."

"Hmm—"

Reid interrupted Jaxon's hum with a brush of lips that progressed to a tender kiss. Not ravenous like their previous efforts, this kiss was sweet as sugar, warm as an August sun. It was the type of kiss that belonged on a tropical beach, where it would taste of coconut and rum, or perhaps in front of a crackling fire with snow falling thickly and frosting the windows. But they were in a basement in Starograd, and that would have to do.

Reid took his time with the kiss, and eventually Jaxon was a little dizzy from lack of oxygen—not that he wanted Reid to stop. Asphyxiation via snogging was much preferable to being caught by Talmirov's men. But even better was when Reid tugged off Jaxon's T-shirt and pressed warm lips to Jaxon's chest. Reid lavished attention on Jaxon's nipples, making him moan greedily, and then he traced the tattoo with his tongue before licking his way down to Jaxon's belly. He lapped at Jaxon's skin like a connoisseur tasting caviar.

At first, Jaxon had clutched Reid's shoulders, but as the careful attention continued, he let his body go lax. He focused entirely on Reid's palms resting just over his hips and on the points of contact with Reid's mouth—hot and soft and maddeningly delicate.

The sensation was so wonderful that he almost complained when Reid shifted slightly and pulled Jaxon's pants and underwear past his thighs. Almost complained but not quite, because what came next was even better: Reid's mouth on the points of his hips, on the creases where his legs met torso, on the tender skin over his balls, and then, praise all that was holy, on the head of his cock.

Jaxon had been on the receiving end of plenty of blowjobs, but none of them had been as excruciatingly slow and intense as this one. Reid would swallow him to the root, and just when Jaxon had almost reached his climax, Reid would back off and give teasing little licks here and there. It occurred to Jaxon that this might be an advanced torture technique Reid had picked up in spy school.

"You're... killing me," Jaxon panted after the zillionth time Reid backed off.

Reid managed an evil chuckle, even with his mouth full. Talented man. But then perhaps he took pity on Jaxon, because he licked his dick from root to tip, placed a tender kiss right on the crown, and rasped, "Let it go, Jax." Then he took the entire length inside his throat, and this time he didn't stop. In fact, he made a deep groaning noise that Jaxon felt more than he heard, and that was it. Jaxon came hard enough to see sparks.

And Reid? He wasn't through. He licked Jaxon tenderly, somehow not irritating his oversensitized skin. He placed more gentle kisses on Jaxon's balls and soft cock before pulling up his clothes. Then he scooted up for an intimate mouth-to-mouth kiss. Tasting himself on Reid's tongue was almost too heady to bear.

Several minutes passed before Jaxon was capable of speech. "Let me up so I can return the favor."

Reid's laugh rumbled against Jaxon's cheek. "No need."

With some difficulty Jaxon squeezed his hand between their bodies and down the front of Reid's pants. Reid's groin was wet and sticky.

"Wow," Jaxon said. He'd been so caught up in what Reid had been doing to him that he hadn't noticed what Reid was doing to himself. "You enjoyed it too."

"I did. Jax?" An odd tentativeness entered his tone. "I don't do this often. Sex, I mean. It gets in the way."

"I have sex a lot—as I'm sure you know. But not like this."

"Not in secret basement hideaways?"

Jaxon gave Reid's ass a healthy squeeze. "Not with someone I... know. Someone who's under my skin. You want to know something else? I think I'm more scared of you than I am of Talmirov and all his minions."

Reid propped himself up to look at Jaxon's face. In the dim light of the single bulb, Jaxon could barely see his concerned frown. "Scared? I've been honest with you about the mission priority, but I won't hurt you."

"I'm pretty sure you won't stab or poison me," Jaxon replied with a bitter chuckle. "But I think you're going to hurt me."

Reid sighed and nestled back against him. "I've made myself into a weapon. That's all I know how to do."

Chapter Twelve

THE secret knock startled them awake, and in their haste to detangle, Reid almost ended up on the floor. But he scrambled to his feet and attended to the door while Jaxon stood and stretched and doubted the wisdom of two grown men sleeping on one narrow couch. Still, despite the crick in his neck and ache in his lower back, he wouldn't have traded the previous night for all the platinum records in the world.

Only three people joined them that morning; the rest, including Fedir, had to work. But Lera and her colleagues brought bread and yogurt and something akin to prosciutto. They tried to apologize for the modest meal, but with Reid interpreting, Jaxon made it clear he was grateful for the food and even more so for the sanctuary. He wasn't hungry anyway, not with worry gnawing at his belly.

After eating and a quick wash-up, Reid spent a bit of time looking over hand-drawn maps. He seemed only mildly satisfied with what he saw.

Finally, he turned to Jaxon with a grim expression. "If I don't make it—"

"Stop. I know what I'm supposed to do."

"Okay."

"Good luck."

Reid tried to smile. "Aren't you supposed to tell me to break a leg?"

"Just don't get yourself killed."

"I'll try to avoid it. Do me a favor?"

Jaxon nodded, expecting more instructions on how to evade evil dictators.

But Reid was chewing his lip and avoiding Jaxon's eyes. "Maybe... write a song for me someday?"

"Yeah," Jaxon replied through a tight throat. From now on, possibly *all* his songs would be for Reid. He just hoped like hell they wouldn't be elegies.

Lora was checking her watch impatiently. Clearly it was time for Reid to go, but he just stood there. Then he rushed forward, grabbed Jaxon, and held him in a tight embrace. "Stay safe," Reid whispered. After one more squeeze, he let go.

A moment later, Jaxon was alone.

HE tried hard to keep his mind occupied, but his options were few. Pacing didn't work. He found some printed-and-stapled papers that reminded him of pre-internet zines, but they were in Vasnytsian and he couldn't puzzle out the words. He attempted a sort of sponge bath and had to stop when it reminded him too much of Reid's touch. He explored the basement's nooks and crannies but found little besides empty bottles, a few spiders, and a tiny closet containing another old guitar and a broken violin. None of these things could chase away his vivid mental images of Reid captured, tortured, poisoned, shot.

Even music helped only a little. He strummed away, humming a few old tunes, yet his heart wasn't in it and all the notes sounded flat. So he ended up composing a new song instead, a searing little piece about people who suffered from iron fists while struggling toward open palms. He didn't write down the lyrics but was confident he'd remember them. He hoped someday he'd get to perform the song for Fedir and his friends.

Loud knocks in the familiar pattern startled him, and he ran to the door, wondering how much time had passed since Reid left. It felt like centuries. When he unbolted the door, he encountered two of the men from the night before. But since he hadn't chatted with them, he didn't remember their names. Last night they'd smiled and sung along with him; today they were pale and wide-eyed.

Neither one of them, it turned out, spoke English. Their rapid Vasnytsian was accompanied by hand gestures to make their meaning clear. They wanted Jaxon to go with them.

He hesitated in the doorway, heart pounding. "What's happened with Reid? Is he all right? Did he make it safely?"

They didn't understand. One handed him a blue woolen cap, and the other gave him a grimy set of coveralls. When Jaxon was dressed, he asked again, "But Reid?"

When the men shook their heads, he hoped it meant they couldn't communicate, not that hope was lost.

The shorter one grasped Jaxon's arm and gave an urgent tug. Obviously they had to leave.

Jaxon kept his head bowed as he hurried up the stairs. The Black Cat had few customers, and soon he was outside and being ushered into a truck, where the men had him crouch in the passenger footwell. They sat on the bench seat, the taller one revved the engine to life, and they rumbled down the street.

They could be taking him anywhere. Maybe they were traitors to the people's cause—or simply worried he'd harm the resistance movement—and planned to deliver him to Talmirov. Or maybe they'd just dump him somewhere far from their hideout, where Jaxon would be helpless. He couldn't even read the street signs. *Real* spies, men like Reid, surely didn't sit passively, just hoping they didn't puke.

The truck cab reeked of old cigarette smoke, and the vehicle bounced and squealed as it drove over rough cobblestones and potholed pavement. The driver and other passenger remained silent, their bodies tight with tension. Every time the truck turned a corner, Jaxon jostled against the passenger's legs and bashed the back of his head on the underside of the dashboard. He stared down at the floorboards, where bits of trash and dirt were embedded in the metal and fabric and plastic, and he wondered at the twists of fate that had delivered him here. It was still better than worrying about what the hell had happened to Reid.

What would the people back in Peril think if they knew where Jaxon was now? And his parents? He hadn't spoken to them in years. He used to try to send them money, but they never cashed the checks, so eventually he gave up. He sent them a Christmas card every damn year, though, and they sent one too. They mailed it to Buzz, since that was Jaxon's only stable address.

Jesus. Buzz. How much had he known of the real purpose of this trip? Jaxon trusted him and knew he wouldn't have endangered him on purpose. How long until he knew Jaxon was missing, and what would he do about it? Jaxon pictured Buzz marching to the State Department in one of his technicolor suits and demanding the rescue of his star client. The image comforted Jaxon a bit—although the realization that his agent was likely the only person on the planet who'd miss him was sobering. Oh, the fans would be sad too. People would post memorial memes on social media and buy Jaxon Powers T-shirts; his music sales would skyrocket. Maybe he'd even get a tribute band. *That* was fucking depressing.

Reid. Reid. Goddammit, what had happened to Reid?

The truck picked up speed. When Jaxon risked a glance out a window, he caught a glimpse of greenery and realized they must be heading out of the city. Maybe they were going north to the border Reid had tried to cross. Jaxon hunched in on himself more tightly and tried to remember prayers from his childhood, but nothing came to him but music. Fine. His songs were sometimes prayers too. He hummed quietly, allowing the engine's rumble to drown him out.

As the truck slowed abruptly, Jaxon's companions erupted into a flurry of what had to be Vasnytsian swearing. The passenger tapped Jaxon's shoulder and patted the seat between him and the driver. Once Jaxon was properly seated, he received lots of instructions. He didn't understand a word.

But what he saw through the windshield made him react so strongly that he probably wouldn't have understood English either. They were on a two-lane road, badly pitted and lined with trees and thick undergrowth. Directly ahead, a jeep-like vehicle with official-looking insignia blocked half the road. The other half was occupied by three uniformed men with guns.

Jaxon would have felt a lot better if the driver hadn't seemed to be mumbling prayers.

The truck came to a complete stop just short of the roadblock, but the driver kept the engine running. As the soldiers sauntered over, Jaxon did his best to look like a bored but obedient Vasnytsian worker. He kept his head ducked in what he hoped was a nonfurtive way. One of the soldiers approached the driver's side while the other two, smoking and looking bored, remained in front of the truck.

The closer soldier barked a command, and the driver handed over a sheaf of papers in grimy plastic covers, which the soldier appeared to skim through. He handed them back and demanded something else. The man to Jaxon's right reached across to give the soldier more documents. Again a quick scan before they were returned.

Then the soldier barked something else, paused, and repeated himself angrily. Jaxon dared a glance and was horrified to realize the soldier was talking to him. When the driver tried to intervene, the soldier yelled at him. The driver shouted back. The other two soldiers began to walk closer.

Unseen by anyone but Jaxon, the driver slowly reached under his seat.

But before he could get what he was grasping for—a gun?—a voice called loudly from the jeep's radio. All three soldiers turned to look. And Jaxon's driver hit the gas.

Letting out an undignified squawk, Jaxon thudded painfully into the other passenger. Before Jaxon could even brace himself, the driver pulled out a handgun from under the seat and fired several shots at the jeep. He was a good driver and a hell of a marksman, because even as the truck roared away, a geyser of steam erupted from the jeep's hood. Jaxon's companions shouted at each other; Jaxon just held on to the seat and closed his eyes.

Eventually the truck slowed and turned into a narrow lane, where dense tree branches scraped the roof. The driver stopped and cut the engine. With impressive speed but no dignity, Jaxon scrambled over the passenger, opened the door, and fell onto the ground, where he proceeded to spew the contents of his stomach onto the dirt.

SOMEWHAT later Jaxon felt a little better. His new friends—taller Spartak was the driver, shorter Oles the passenger—gave him a bottle of water to rinse his mouth and clean himself up a bit.

At least Jaxon was now fairly certain that Spartak and Oles were on his side and not planning to turn him over to the authorities. But Jesus, they'd almost been caught. He should have known how serious this was— he'd seen Albina die, Mariya had disappeared, and he had no clue as to Reid's fate. Somehow none of those things had driven it home like hearing bullets fly.

Apparently satisfied that Jaxon was through puking, Oles walked over to Jaxon, who was slumped on the grass. He gave Jaxon's shoulder a friendly pat and pointed at the truck.

"Time to go?" asked Jaxon as he rose to his feet, and Oles answered something in Vasnytsian. As Jaxon settled into the middle of the seat, he vowed that if he survived this adventure, he'd never travel to another country without at least a smattering of the language and a decent phrasebook.

Spartak backed out of the leafy lane and then kept the truck rolling at a brisk pace over narrow roads, perhaps trying to avoid the main routes. They passed forests, farmland, and several small and run-down villages. Sometimes Jaxon caught a glimpse of a factory belching smoke in the distance, usually with a nearby collection of rabbit-hutch apartments, but Spartak stayed away from those larger settlements. They saw few other vehicles.

Jaxon had fallen into a light doze when Spartak stopped the truck in the middle of a heavy copse and cut the engine. With the sky darkening to twilight, Jaxon, Spartak, and Oles walked a footpath that wound past ancient stone walls and ruined houses. Jaxon couldn't tell what had destroyed the houses or how long ago. They skirted another stand of trees and walked up a steep hill. A castle stood there, smaller than the one in Starograd but in much better shape. Although it had an air of neglect, at least its walls and roof were intact.

Pointing at the castle, Oles said something, and this time Jaxon actually caught one of the words: Turks. This must have been a defensive fortress from the days of the Ottoman Empire.

Birds were settling into the nearby treetops, doing a last call to one another, and the waning moon had become visible through sparse clouds. Jaxon followed Oles and Spartak through the castle's arched entryway and into a bare courtyard. Someone waved at them from a second-story balcony, but Jaxon couldn't see much of her except long brown hair. Spartak knocked on a wooden door—more Rolling Stones—which opened at once into a large room with walls and floor of smooth stone. Lera was there, and she and Jaxon's companions began talking rapidly. But Jaxon's attention narrowed to what he saw across the room: a woman who knelt over a blanket-covered figure lying on the ground. All that was visible of the shrouded mass was a familiar crew cut of dark hair.

Chapter Thirteen

JAXON didn't remember crossing the large room. One moment he stood just inside the doorway, staring in horror at Reid's still body, and the next moment he was falling to his knees and reaching for Reid's face.

"Do not—" began the woman, but it was too late for whatever warning she wanted to give. Jaxon touched his palm to one stubbled cheek, and Reid opened his eyes.

"Jax." Reid's voice was hoarse but strong. He grabbed Jaxon's hand with enough strength to prove his vitality. "You're here."

Jaxon felt light-headed with relief. But then he saw the raw scrapes on Reid's forehead and the bloody bandage on his other hand. "What's wrong? What happened? You're hurt!"

"I failed. Tried to sneak over the border and fucked up."

"But what's wrong with you?" Jaxon wanted to tear away the blanket and inspect Reid himself, but the woman was blocking him.

Reid shook his head. "I'll be fine. I'm just—" His eyes narrowed then widened. "You look like shit. Are you—"

"I'm fine."

"The hell you are."

A skirmish followed, with Jaxon trying to get information from Reid, Reid trying to interrogate Jaxon, and the woman doing her best to keep them separated. They finally came to a truce, in which Jaxon and Reid stayed close, kept their hands to themselves, and took turns with their stories. Jaxon went first, to the accompaniment of assorted swearing by Reid. The woman—whose name was Gertruda and who was some kind of doctor—interjected a few exclamations as well. Neither of them was happy to hear about the encounter with the soldiers.

"But you're okay?" Reid asked when the tale was told.

"I barfed spectacularly and almost pissed my pants, but I'm fine. You're not, though."

Reid winced as he squirmed around a bit. "The border guards saw me and started shooting—"

"Reid!"

"They didn't hit me. Poorly trained. But it's rough terrain and I took a nasty fall while I was retreating. Luckily I'd lost the guards by then, so they couldn't scoop me up, but I banged myself up pretty good."

"How good?" demanded Jaxon.

"Don't think I broke anything, but I've got some deep bruising and a lot of abrasions."

"He needs to rest," Gertruda said with a scowl. With her short gray hair and solid build, she was a formidable-looking woman. She might have been a couple of decades older than Jaxon, but she probably could have taken him in a fight.

Reid patted her hand. "He's going to pester until he gets his answers, so you might as well get it over with. He's a stubborn ass." He said the last bit with a degree of fondness.

Pressing his advantage, Jaxon asked, "How did you get here?"

"The wonders of technology. Lera gave me an RFID chip so she could monitor my progress. When her scanner showed me moving away from the border really fast and then abruptly stopping, she figured something had happened and came to my rescue."

Jaxon added Lera to the list of people he wanted to thank in song someday. "So now what?"

"I don't know. I'll be able to move by tomorrow, I think, but they'll have doubled down on border security. After your adventure they'll be crawling all over the roads too. Maybe if we can lie low for a little while…." But Reid looked skeptical.

And if Reid didn't have any bright ideas how to get out of this mess, Jaxon sure as hell didn't. Not only was he not James Bond, but his head was so muddled with the day's events he could barely remember his own name. Surprisingly, he also felt a thread of gratitude. He and Reid were still alive and kicking. Or, more accurately, alive and lying on the floor.

Gertruda clucked at him. "Rest," she told Jaxon as she rearranged Reid's pillow.

"I'm wiped, but just give me a minute, okay? Maybe near-death experiences are commonplace for you guys, but they're a new thing for me." Jaxon turned to Reid. "How come we saw only three soldiers? Not that I'm complaining, but I'd have expected a bigger roadblock. And those three weren't very good at it." Getting distracted by a radio was a poor strategy.

Reid seemed to consider this for a moment. "I think they're all badly trained. They've been drafted and they get paid next to nothing, so they may not be strongly motivated to do their duty." A groan when he shifted again. "And I think Talmirov underestimates the opposition. He has no idea how close things are to tipping away from him. Narcissists are like that— they believe everyone loves them as much as they love themselves."

While Jaxon was contemplating that, Oles approached and held out a plate of bread and sliced meat. Although Jaxon's only meal of the day hadn't stayed with him, he wasn't hungry. Too exhausted, too worried, too traumatized. Too everything. So he shook his head. "No thanks. I really just want to sleep."

Reid translated, and Oles nodded knowingly. He took the food away and returned shortly with a blanket and a stack of newspapers. Gertruda helped Jaxon spread the newspapers into a makeshift mat, and she didn't even complain when he insisted on sleeping within arm's reach of Reid. He wrapped himself in the blanket, and with the murmur of Vasnytsian conversation nearby and Reid's steady gaze trained on him, Jaxon swiftly fell asleep.

HE didn't sleep well. Despite the newspapers, the stone floor was hard, and the room was drafty. And noisy too. The building emitted creaks and moans, and although the other people tried to keep their conversations low, their voices carried. When he managed to catch a little sleep, he had unsettling dreams of being chased, of falling, of guns firing. Then he would awaken to worry about Reid, who moaned periodically through the night.

When the first weak light of dawn crept in through the windows, Jaxon stood and joined Oles in the courtyard. Oles smiled and, after heating water over a small fire, made Jaxon some coffee. Jaxon drank it gratefully and ate a roll Oles produced from somewhere.

"Are you going to be okay?" Jaxon asked him.

But Oles didn't understand any of the question except *okay*, which he echoed, then shrugged. Fuck. Jaxon didn't know a thing about this man who'd risked his own life to help him and who was now probably a fugitive too. Did he have family? What made him join the resistance? What were his hopes for the future?

The castle did not have plumbing, so Jaxon had to make do with a nearby tree and then a bucket of water Oles drew from a cistern. With eyes still sleep-grimy, Jaxon went back inside the room, where he was happy to see Reid standing upright. For once, Reid didn't look dapper. He was shirtless, his back slightly hunched, his torso dotted with bandages and mottled with bruises.

"Should you be moving around?" Jaxon asked as he hurried over. He looked around for Gertruda, but she wasn't there.

"Can't stay here."

"Then where are we going? Oh, and note the *we*, because we're not splitting up again."

It was a sign of Reid's diminished state that he sighed instead of arguing. "I don't know."

"What about the other borders? Can we try them?"

"No. They were always better protected than the north, and now…."

Shit. "There must be some way for you to get word to your people."

"I can't just send them a goddamn text message!" Reid winced. "Sorry. I didn't mean to…. There are ways to get messages out, but they're slow and risky in themselves. We don't have the time. And it's pointless anyway because they can't extract us."

Not caring at this point whether anyone was watching, Jaxon moved closer and rested a hand on Reid's shoulder, carefully avoiding a large scratch. "You'll think of something."

"Really? My mind's a fucking blank right now."

"Because you're tired and you hurt. And when did you eat last? Give yourself some time."

"Might as well tell me to give myself a platypus."

Jaxon blinked at him. "Huh?"

"Don't have a platypus; don't have time."

"Let me get you some breakfast." Jaxon was beginning to wonder if Reid was showing symptoms of a concussion.

Reid waved a hand dismissively. "I'll get it. Have to piss anyway." His gait was slower and more uneven than usual, but he made it out of the room on his own steam. Although tempted to follow, Jaxon remained inside. Sometimes a guy needed space.

Jaxon paced the large room, nodding at the Vasnytsians who sat in a corner playing cards. He wondered what the original purpose of the space had been. A meeting hall, perhaps? The room contained several broken wall sconces and two enormous fireplaces empty of everything but ancient soot. Had Vasnytsians gathered here once upon a time for dinners, and if so, had musicians entertained them?

As soon as that question crossed Jaxon's mind, so did the image of a medieval singer huddled in a cold castle on a winter night, waiting for the battle at dawn. But he wasn't scared, because his lover—a soldier— had been killed in the last fight, and now the musician yearned to join him. Shit. Jaxon knew exactly the words to write, and the tune was already playing in his head. He used sign language to beg a pen and a few scraps of paper from one of the men in the room, and then Jaxon sat on his makeshift bed, scribbling frantically.

"What are you writing?"

Jaxon startled. He hadn't noticed Reid's return, and now he loomed over him. But at least Reid was looking more chipper, which cheered Jaxon a bit. "I just got an idea for a song."

"They come to you just like that?"

"Sure. Sometimes when I'm fooling around with my guitar, but other times too. Especially when I'm in the shower, for some reason."

Reid carefully lowered himself to his bed. "I can't play any instruments, I can't carry a tune, and I couldn't write a decent anything if my life depended on it."

"But you could save people if *their* lives depended on it. In the end, James Bond's more useful than Elvis Presley."

"Elvis has a lot more fans."

Jaxon pointed the pen at him. "But Bond's pretty popular with the ladies."

"I don't want Pussy Galore."

Jaxon laughed hard, and even Reid cracked a smile. But then someone outside shouted in Vasnytsian, and Reid shot to his feet with a speed that would have been impressive even for an uninjured man. He looked chagrined when he reached for a weapon and realized he remained shirtless.

"What is it?" Jaxon stood with less rapidity.

Reid was looking around for something lethal. "Someone's coming."

A few minutes later, though, the voice called out again, followed by a familiar knock on the door. Reid relaxed. "Friends."

In fact, the newcomers turned out to be Fedir and a frizzy-haired woman Jaxon remembered from the Black Cat. She waved at him and headed straight to the card players, who'd taken up arms when the alarm was sounded. Fedir walked over to Jaxon and Reid.

"You have been busy," Fedir said to them. He frowned slightly at Reid. "And you are hurt."

Reid waved impatiently. "What's going on out there? Any news?"

"People know something is wrong. They are...." Fedir said a Vasnytsian word.

"Uneasy," Reid translated. "Have there been announcements from the government?"

"No, no, of course not. But more police, more soldiers on streets. And second concert is cancelled. Officials say Jaxon is sick, but nobody believes this."

The Workers' Day concert—Jaxon had completely forgotten about it. He did a calculation in his head and realized it was supposed to happen the following night. Some fans would surely be disappointed, and he felt bad about that even though he couldn't avoid it. "I wish there was some way for me to apologize to everyone."

Fedir clapped his back. "Someday people will know what you did for us. You will be hero."

"I haven't done anything. Reid's the hero."

"Two heroes," said Fedir with a grin.

Reid clearly didn't care who was a hero. "Have you had any luck at finding a way to decode and send the documents on the chip?"

"No. Maybe someday soon, but not now. Now we find you safe place."

"Where?"

"I do not know. But I think…." After a pause and a grimace, Fedir lapsed into Vasnytsian while pointing at the people in the corner. He stopped long enough to shrug at Jaxon. "I am sorry. My English is not good enough."

"Don't apologize, dude. We're in your country. If you guys want to scheme, go ahead. I won't be any help anyway."

They took him at his word, and Jaxon felt only a little left out as everyone else conversed loudly in the corner. He sat back down with his paper and pen. Maybe his fictional singer felt left out too, knowing a mere entertainer wasn't much use in battle—although he was just as much at risk of getting killed as the soldiers.

By the time Reid returned, Jaxon had finished the song and was leaning against the wall, reminiscing. For no particular reason, he'd suddenly remembered the summer when he was twelve and his parents had taken him on a road trip to the Black Hills. They'd stayed at a dumpy old motel and eaten greasy hamburgers, and they'd tromped around Mount Rushmore and Deadwood. It was the first time Jaxon saw real forests and hills taller than the gentle rolling wheat fields of western Nebraska. And yes, it was only South Dakota, but it proved that a world existed outside Peril. Which had been a relief, since he was beginning to realize he'd never fit into his hometown.

"What are you thinking about?" Reid asked, sitting beside him.

"Buffalo and prairie dogs."

"Not platypuses?"

"Those too. Have you solved all our problems?"

"No." Reid shifted closer to him. "Most of them think it's better if we go back to Starograd—more places to hide. But we'd also put more people in danger there. They're throwing around a bunch of plans, but every one of them is a long shot. I don't know what to do, Jax."

Jaxon knew the admission must have been difficult for a man like Reid, yet Jaxon couldn't find the right words of comfort. "Do you want to hear my new song?"

Reid's smile was small but genuine. "Yes. I'd like that a lot."

So Jaxon began to sing. He tried to keep his voice soft, but the acoustics were good, and anyway he swiftly lost himself in the emotions and forgot to stay quiet. Everyone else came over to listen—hesitantly at first, until he nodded them closer—and although Fedir was likely the only one who understood the words, they all seemed carried by the music. Including Reid. He sat completely still, hands steepled near his face as if he were praying. The song itself was different from Jaxon's usual style, a plaintive ballad rather than a roar. Although he wished he had a guitar to accompany him, it worked well a cappella.

When the final echoes of his voice died away, a hushed silence fell. Then his little audience broke into applause and bilingual acclaim. Fedir wiped tears from his eyes. "Beautiful."

But Reid appeared pained, as if his injuries had become worse. "Jesus Christ," he said. And repeated it. "Jesus Christ."

"What?"

"It'll be a fucking tragedy if you never play that onstage."

Jaxon should have been appalled at this admission of possible imminent doom. Instead he leapt to his feet. "I will!" he exclaimed.

"That's a nice sentiment, but—"

"Not a sentiment. A fact. I'm gonna do that concert tomorrow."

Grunting softly, Reid struggled to stand. "That's crazy."

"No, no, listen. We're probably fucked anyway, right? So why not go out with a bang? If the concert comes as a surprise, I might get through a few songs before Talmirov's goons show up. Which might be kinda fun for folks who don't get a lot of fun. Plus it'll make Talmirov look bad—he'll be caught in a lie since I'm obviously not sick."

"But you won't be able to escape like that."

"Big deal. I'm not gonna escape anyway. So maybe they'll shoot me, which is hard to hide if you've got hundreds of witnesses, and it'll also make Talmirov look bad. Or they haul me away to their prison or torture chambers or whatever. Another public black mark for good old Bogdan, and better than if they do it in secret."

Although Reid was shaking his head, he also looked contemplative, as if he were considering Jaxon's words. Meanwhile, Fedir was talking rapidly to his friends, and they showed growing excitement.

"We can help," Fedir announced. "We can tell people. Words move fast in Starograd—we are city built on secrets and whispers. People will come."

"Will they be safe?" asked Jaxon, who didn't want to trigger a bloody revolution.

Fedir shrugged. "We are never safe here." He turned to one of his colleagues for a brief discussion, then nodded and turned back. "Also, we can try something. People can bring mobile phones." He pulled out his flip phone and tapped it meaningfully.

"How will that help?" asked Reid.

"We take pictures. We, uh, catch sound, yes? And maybe some friends will make internet work—then we send to whole world."

"Make the internet work? What do you mean by that?"

As Fedir explained in Vasnytsian, Jaxon took it as a good sign that Reid nodded and looked increasingly more excited. "What?" demanded Jaxon when Fedir was done.

"They have hackers." Reid said it in the same tone Buzz used when the newest Fluevog shoes came in.

"Okaaay?"

"They have a key generator they've stolen from the military, and they can use that to hack into the government's internet connection. I hope. Once that's a go, they can create a Wi-Fi hotspot, and everyone with a flip phone can use the Wi-Fi to upload photos, video, audio— whatever they can manage."

Jaxon didn't know what a key generator was, but he got the gist of what Reid was talking about. "How will this help?"

"It won't help us—you and me, I mean. Talmirov's people will catch on and shut things down fast, and then we—"

"We're fucked. I know. But it helps the cause?"

"With luck." Reid rubbed his mouth. "Whatever people here can get out, it might go viral. Especially with Jaxon Powers standing front and center. Everyone's going to take notice."

Jaxon wasn't used to thinking about schemes and intrigues. Hell, he'd always sucked at chess. "I guess it'll be satisfying to know people are watching on YouTube, but I still don't get how that's going to help the Vasnytsians. That chip's still gonna be in your arm."

"Yeah, this is second-best to getting that data into the right hands, but it might do the trick. People believe what they see and hear, Jax. If *you* tell them Talmirov's corrupt, that he's in bed with Russia, you won't even need the proof. They believe, and suddenly there's a lot of pressure on Western governments to do something. And there's a lot of sympathy for Fedir and his colleagues, which will help a lot."

Fedir nodded his agreement. "Right now, I think nobody cares about us. Why should they? You will make them care."

This wasn't a responsibility Jaxon had asked for. Or expected. Like most of the musicians he knew, he began his career wanting fame and fortune. He wanted people to admire him. He wanted to be more than that weird queer kid, the loner whose own parents had no idea what to do with him. Through some talent and enormous strokes of luck, he'd accomplished all of that. But he'd never dreamed of carrying enough influence to topple a regime.

"With great power comes great responsibility," he muttered.

Reid huffed a laugh. "Peter Parker's not a redhead."

"And I'm not a big fan of spiders. But the principle holds."

"Yes, I guess it does. Are you certain you want to do this? We might come up with another plan."

"You might. But this one'll do the trick, right? It'll fulfill the mission." Jaxon smiled to show he wasn't teasing or being ironic. Somewhere along the line Reid's mission had truly become Jaxon's as well. "I want to do this."

Reid shocked Jaxon with a quick, fierce hug. It was firm enough to make Reid groan, but despite the discomfort, he didn't let go right away. Instead he whispered in Jaxon's ear, "You're a revelation." Then he kissed Jaxon's cheek and released him.

"What's so revelatory about me?"

Reid just shook his head. "We have some planning to do...."

"So I should go play and let the grown-ups work. I got it. I'll plan my set list for tomorrow."

"You're not going to get a chance to do much singing."

"I know. But it'll be fun to come up with a list anyway. The only stop in my Go Out With a Bang Tour." He leaned in and planted a kiss on Reid's cheek.

Chapter Fourteen

IT didn't take Jaxon long to devise the list of songs he wanted to play, but inevitably wouldn't, thanks to Talmirov's minions. He hoped he'd at least manage one or two. He decided to start with the new one, which he was calling "Battle Song." Then maybe he'd follow up with one of his tunes about Nebraska. That seemed fitting: to end his career back, figuratively speaking, where he'd begun.

With Reid still deep in conversation, Jaxon grew bored. He found a stash of cheese sandwiches someone had brought, ate one, and washed it down with a bottled beer. A little exploration was in order, so he left through a doorway at one end of the room and wandered throughout the castle's lower level. There wasn't really much to see; the rooms stood empty except for bits of unidentifiable refuse. Overall the structure was in good condition, which suggested someone had used it after the Ottoman Empire receded. Under vastly different circumstances, Jaxon would have considered buying the property and having it fixed up and modernized so he could live there. If today's experience was anything to judge by, the castle would be an inspirational place to compose music.

"Not gonna happen," Jaxon reminded himself as he climbed a curved stone stairway. It was too bad, really, considering this was the first urge he'd had to settle down.

An interior balcony ran the entire perimeter of the upper floor, providing a view into the central courtyard. One of the Vasnytsians from the Black Cat stood at the balcony railing, apparently chain-smoking. Like a Wild West desperado, she had a pair of pistols holstered around her hips. She smiled at Jaxon and gave him a thumbs-up.

Across the courtyard, the castle's sole tower rose an additional two stories. Jaxon saw the outline of another person inside, keeping an eye out for intruders. If Jaxon owned the castle, he'd put a comfy love seat in the tower and sit there on stormy days, watching the rain come down. It would be nice to have someone special sitting with him.

The upper-floor rooms proved slightly more interesting since they contained a larger and more diverse collection of junk. Some of the plastered walls had ghostly vestiges of murals, the paint too faded to make out details. One room held shards of broken dishes, some of them delicate porcelain but most rougher terra-cotta. Another contained an enormous tiled stove in good condition, its yellow-green glazed tiles decorated with mythological figures. It would have originally burned wood or coal, but he bet it could be adapted for gas, creating a pleasant refuge on a cold winter day.

"Set lists you'll never perform, castle improvement plans you'll never implement. Face reality, Powers." Yet he didn't heed his own lecture; he continued his tour, imagining what he could do with all the rooms.

By the time he made his way back downstairs, the meeting had broken up. Some of the conspirators had returned to playing cards, but Reid sat on his narrow pallet, his gaze faraway.

"What were you up to?" he asked when Jaxon sat beside him.

"Snooping. It's a nice castle."

"I suppose it is."

"Hey, Reid? If I write a couple of letters, is there any chance they might get to people in the US? Eventually?"

"There's always a chance." Reid didn't look optimistic.

Jaxon grabbed paper and pen. The first letter was for Buzz, and it was fairly easy to write. Jaxon thanked him for representing him so well and being instrumental in his success. He said he'd like his wealth to be donated to good causes—Buzz could choose which ones—and Buzz could own the rights to Jaxon's name and music. He trusted Buzz to make good decisions. Jaxon wasn't sure if the letter would be legally binding, but since he'd never bothered to write a will, he figured it was worth a try. No use letting the lawyers leach everything away.

He folded the paper and wrote Buzz's name, address, and email on the outside. Then he remained still for a long time, pen in hand. Finally he wrote:

Dear Mom and Dad,

I'm sorry I was never the son you wanted. I know it's been hard on you. I wish you could have accepted me the way I am. But I appreciate what you did for me, and I love you. I hope I made you proud of me in the end.

Love,

Jaxon

He seriously considered signing it with the original spelling of his name, but that felt as if he was selling himself out. He'd been Jaxon-with-an-x for a long time now, and that's who he wanted to be.

"Do you want to write any letters?" Jaxon held the remaining papers toward Reid.

"No."

That hurt. "There's nobody…?"

"I knew what I was signing up for when I took this job."

That didn't explain why Reid was so alone in the world, but Jaxon didn't push it. He didn't want them to fight, not now.

After a while Reid took Jaxon's letters to one of the people in the corner, who nodded and tucked them into a pocket. Then Reid returned to the bed, wincing as he sat down. "As soon as it gets dark, we're leaving."

"Where to?"

"Starograd. Safer than trying to travel there during the day."

"All right. But we're going together, right?"

"Yes."

That, at least, was a small relief.

AS Reid promised, they left the castle shortly after nightfall. Jaxon and Reid squished together in the back of a panel truck that smelled of cabbages and grease. Someone had hastily jerry-rigged a secret compartment in the cargo area, immediately behind the seats. It had just enough space for two men to sit, and while it wouldn't pass careful scrutiny, it was better than no camouflage at all.

The ride was uncomfortable for Jaxon and obviously painful for Reid. Although Jaxon couldn't see him in the dark, he heard him moan at the bigger bumps. "Come here," Jaxon ordered after a particularly large bang. He tugged at Reid's arm.

"What?" Reid sounded irritable.

"Turn around and lean back against me. I can be your shock absorber."

"I don't need—"

"Don't martyr yourself. No reason to suffer more than necessary."

Grumbling, Reid obeyed. With grunts and muttered profanities, he repositioned himself until he was sitting between Jaxon's legs and leaning his back against Jaxon's chest. That put his hair in front of Jaxon's nose. It tickled and carried the odors of earth, cigarette smoke, and antiseptic, but Jaxon didn't mind. Feeling slightly silly, he hummed some favorite songs, and Reid relaxed against him so thoroughly that Jaxon suspected he'd fallen asleep.

Twice the truck halted. Loud voices shouted commands, and someone opened the back of the truck. But although Jaxon's heart beat prestissimo and Reid's body tensed as he readied himself for attack, nobody disturbed their hideaway, and the truck soon started rolling again.

Jaxon was dozing when the truck made a third stop. Reid went rigid as the back door rattled open and someone began pulling at the entrance to their compartment.

Relief made Jaxon giddy as friendly, familiar faces greeted them. He offered Reid a hand to help him stand—Jaxon was pretty stiff himself—but Reid ignored it.

They'd stopped in a weedy parking lot at the center of several rabbit-hutch apartment buildings. Only a few other vehicles were there, and they looked like Yugos held together with dental floss and Scotch tape. With small, dimly lit apartment windows as the only sign of life, the place had an eerie postapocalyptic vibe. Moving quickly and without saying a word, the two Vasnytsians who'd driven the truck led them into one of the buildings. The single functioning bulb in the small lobby flickered sporadically. A large potted tree clung desperately to life near a window, flanked by a pair of badly dented metal benches. The air was heavy with the odors of past meals.

One of their companions said something, and Reid translated. "The elevator has cameras. We'll take the stairs."

Fair enough, except it turned out they were going to the sixth floor. By the time they neared it, Reid was pulling himself up by the banister. They walked down a narrow hallway lined with identical doors faintly illuminated by more failing light bulbs, and then one of the Vasnytsians knocked softly on the door at the very end. It opened swiftly and they all went inside, but after a brief conversation, the two men from the truck left.

The middle-aged barista from the Black Cat stood looking at Jaxon and Reid, her gray hair in a bun and her arms crossed over a considerable bosom. She didn't appear thrilled to see them, and she sure wasn't wowed by the famous Jaxon Powers, but she didn't kick them out. She spoke briefly with Reid, gifted Jaxon with another skeptical look, and left the apartment.

"She says there's food in the kitchen," said Reid. "And clothing in the bedroom."

"God, *please* let there be a shower with hot water."

Jaxon's prayer was answered—a little on-demand water heater was attached directly to the shower—but he didn't take advantage right away. He prowled through the apartment first, which didn't take long. A small living room and a smaller bedroom, both stuffed with oversize wooden furniture likely older than his parents, and a kitchen unchanged since the apartment was built in the sixties. The antique refrigerator wheezed like an old man climbing stairs, the stove looked like an electrical fire waiting to happen, and the square table wobbled. But as promised, there was food—bread, sausages, tomatoes, and a dry, nutty cake—and a few bottles of beer. Jaxon and Reid ate heartily.

"Think we can both fit in that shower?" Jaxon asked while helping Reid clean up after the meal.

"I'm barely going to fit by myself."

True enough, if disappointing. "I'm going to supervise. I need to check out your wounds."

Reid snorted. "I doubt that's all you'll be checking out."

"Yeah, yeah."

As soon as Reid undressed, Jaxon actually did examine his injuries. Even though Reid had been shirtless at the castle, the light had been poor, and now Jaxon was able to see the rest of him—lots of big, ugly bruises topped with scrapes and cuts. Reid's injuries looked a lot like Jaxon's had when he was eight years old and, wearing nothing but cutoffs and flip-flops, took a corner too fast on his bike. He'd slid across the pavement and down an embankment before nearly landing on railroad tracks. It had hurt like hell, and his mother had practically drowned him in antiseptic, but he survived. He figured Reid would too. Well, until Talmirov caught them.

Their host had kindly supplied them with soap and shampoo. Jaxon sat on the toilet while Reid used the cramped shower, and although a degree of ogling might have taken place, that wasn't Jaxon's primary motive. He simply didn't want to be separated—not even by a single room—during their remaining time together.

"You have scars," Jaxon observed loudly over the din of the running water. He hadn't had an opportunity to notice them previously, but they dotted and crossed Reid's body like runes.

"Army. State Department."

"You've had a lot of adventures."

"I suppose."

"Were they worth it?"

Reid rinsed the shampoo from his hair before answering. "I guess. I think I've done some good."

"If you could go back in time, would you do it all the same?"

"Doesn't matter. Nobody can go back."

True enough, but it was still an interesting question. "I'd still come here, to Vasnytsia. Knowing what I know now."

Pausing, soap in hand, Reid squinted at him. "That's crazy. If you'd stayed in the States, you'd be at one of your fancy hotels, earning millions of dollars, sleeping with adoring fans."

"Been there, done that."

"You're going to *die*, Jax. Soon. Maybe you'll rot in a prison for a while first, but—"

"I *know*. But my statement stands—I'd do it again."

Apparently concluding that Jaxon was too nuts to converse with, Reid turned his back to him for the rest of the shower. When he was finished, he left the water running, stepped out, and gestured for Jaxon to take his place.

Jaxon expected Reid to leave the bathroom, but he didn't. While Jaxon showered, Reid leaned against the wall with a towel around his waist and waited. The water pressure wasn't great, but it still felt wonderful, and getting truly clean was a treat.

Their host had left toothpaste and new toothbrushes as well. No razors, but that wasn't a big deal. He could do his last gig with stubble. During all the time it took Jaxon to work the tangles out of his hair, Reid watched silently. Jaxon found himself wondering what it would be like to have hair so short that you didn't even need a comb.

They abandoned their old clothing, quickly folded, in the bathroom and found clean clothes in the bedroom—tighty-whities, T-shirts, and tracksuits. Reid's tee was gray, while Jaxon's was white with four clenched fists and a Vasnytsian word, all printed in red ink. "What does it say?"

Reid's mouth twitched into a small smile. "We resist."

"I like that."

"Not as fancy as your usual concert clothes."

"Better than fancy. I don't usually dress up much anyway." He grinned. "Are you doing okay without your suits?"

"I like suits."

Jaxon pulled on his underwear but left the rest of the clothing for the morning. He would have remained naked, but if the army stormed in during the middle of the night, he didn't want *everything* hanging loose.

"But do you like suits because you know you look hot in them or because they're sort of a uniform?" He was willing to bet it was the latter. It was like some of the singers he'd met—they'd pierce their faces, wear locks around their necks, and tease their dyed hair into mohawks, just to make sure everyone know they were punk musicians, dammit. Not that Reid was a poser, but his suits said Important Government Guy.

"I just like them," Reid insisted.

The bedroom held a tall double bed, a shorter single, and an oversized armchair that would have worked for sleeping. But when Jaxon climbed into the bigger bed, Reid joined him minus underwear. Apparently he didn't care whether he flashed the invading military.

Even with their bodies squashed together, Reid made no sexual overtures. And honestly, Jaxon didn't want sex either. He'd had plenty of fucking in his life. Tonight he wanted something... bigger. Like listening to Reid's breathing in the darkness and rubbing his nose against the soft brush of his hair.

He thought Reid had gone to sleep, but then he shifted and exhaled a sigh. "Sometimes I miss them," he said. "My parents."

Treading carefully, Jaxon kept his voice low. "Yeah?"

"We weren't close. They weren't demonstrative types. Me either."

Jaxon gave him a quick hug. "Apparently I have a thing for strong and silent. Anyway, you're demonstrating pretty nicely right now."

"Maybe I can get better with practice. My parents never had the chance—they both died young."

Jaxon guessed that words of comfort wouldn't have been welcome, so he held Reid tighter instead, wrapping his arms around his middle and pulling his back up close to Jaxon's front. He placed a soft kiss on Reid's nape. "You've already made yourself into something damned amazing."

"I just do my job. I'm nothing like those beautiful people you sleep with."

"I don't sleep with them—I fuck them. Not the same thing. And here's the deal. When they come to me, they're not really looking for *me*. They want the superstar, the guy they listen to on iTunes and wear on their T-shirts. I'm a trophy for them. And maybe they want some of my money too, or they hope fame will rub off on them. I don't blame them for it—but it's just a commercial transaction."

"What do you get out of it?"

Jaxon had to think that over. "An itch scratched. A little company and adoration. I don't blame me either."

"Okay."

"You're not just scratching my itches, Reid. And I think I annoy you too much for you to adore me. But God, that under-the-skin thing? You're deeper than that. I think you've worked yourself all the way into my heart."

"Why?" Reid demanded after a moment. "Because I look good in a suit?"

"You look good in anything, but no. Because… when you look at me, I get the feeling you see *me*. Not the rock star."

"I see you," Reid agreed.

"You and I, I think we've both spent our lives bouncing around alone. You put on a uniform to protect yourself, I play my music and float from hotel to hotel. Nobody gets near us, 'cause then they can't hurt us." Jaxon chuckled. "Did your dossier mention that I've spent time in therapy?"

Reid snorted.

After another light kiss, Jaxon continued. "I feel like I can let you near me. You're safe."

"Safe?" Reid squirmed around to face him, although the room was too dark to see much of anything.

"I'm the most dangerous person you know. I'm worse than Talmirov. Without me, he'd have listened to you sing and sent you on home with a pile of money and fabulous parting gifts."

"Nevertheless, I feel safe with you."

Reid growled softly and clutched Jaxon's shoulder. "Don't you get it? We don't get to ride off together into the sunset and decorate a cute little bungalow in Malibu. We have no future."

"Then can we enjoy the now? 'Cause we've got that."

A long silence, followed by a sigh. "Yes, I guess we do."

They made out for a while, kisses deep and tender, but they didn't have sex. Instead Reid asked Jaxon to sing to him, and Jaxon did, the quiet notes surrounding them like cotton clouds. They both knew those clouds would clear in the morning, but for now they felt soft and warm and sweet.

Chapter Fifteen

JAXON didn't need an alarm to wake up early; anxiety did the job quite nicely. But he didn't get up right away, choosing instead to remain in bed and watch Reid sleep. Reid frowned and muttered in his dreams, and Jaxon wondered if his nightmares were about recent events or those from his childhood. Had anyone ever tried to soothe those nightmares away?

During Jaxon's third therapy appointment, Dr. Vega had given him a children's book.

"*The Ugly Duckling*?" Jaxon had asked, turning the slim volume in his hands.

"Read it. We'll talk about it next week."

Although he was bemused, he'd obeyed. And when he and Dr. Vega discussed the reasons why the little swan's family had rejected it, Jaxon had reached a better understanding of his parents and the people in his hometown. They weren't cruel or hateful people; they simply had no idea what to do when fate plopped a swan into their duckish lives. Maybe he'd never entirely forgive them, but he could understand them, could fathom why they'd treated him so poorly, and that had helped his own healing.

Jaxon would have bet his life—what was left of it—that Reid had never been in therapy. Some part of him must blame himself for the mistreatment by his family. Maybe that was why he'd become an intelligence agent, to make up for his imagined sins. But now he also held himself responsible for his mission's failure and Jaxon's predicament. Jaxon wished he could help Reid see his own worth.

But there was no time.

Reid startled awake and stared up at Jaxon. "Why are you looming?" Reid asked groggily.

"I'm thinking about ducks and swans."

"Not platypuses?"

Jaxon smiled and traced Reid's lips with a fingertip.

This time it didn't take an argument to bring them together, and Reid didn't put up even token resistance as Jaxon explored his body with hands and mouth. The only protest came when Jaxon got out of bed. "Where are you—"

"Be right back," Jaxon said and ran to the kitchen, thankful for the apartment's small size. It took only a minute to prepare what he needed.

When Jaxon returned, he came to an abrupt halt in the doorway, breathless at the sight of Reid naked, spread out. Waiting for him.

"What's that?" Reid asked, pointing at Jaxon's hand.

Jaxon grinned and tilted the little dish so Reid could see.

"Butter? You're making breakfast now?"

"I'm offering you breakfast in bed." With a waggle of his brows, Jaxon launched himself onto Reid.

A few pats of butter didn't make the best lube, but it was far better than nothing. Reid seemed to enjoy applying it, and Jaxon liked having it applied. Due to their potentially short futures, safer sex practices seemed unimportant. Besides, it was lovely to have this sexual encounter be entirely skin to skin, a luxury Jaxon had never indulged in. And God, the heat of Reid inside him, the fire in Reid's eyes as he tortured Jaxon with slow thrusts, the salty taste of Reid's skin... those sensations nearly overwhelmed him. Best yet, however, was the aftermath, when they held each other in a sweaty, buttery tangle and felt their slowing heartbeats sync.

"If we weren't doomed," Jaxon whispered, letting the thought hang there, unspoken.

"We'd be doomed anyway. I can't... I never stay put for longer than a few weeks."

"Neither do I."

"Our lives could never mesh, not for long."

Jaxon looked at him solemnly. "I'd retire if it meant I could keep you." Huh. He hadn't consciously realized the truth of those words until he said them out loud. "Would you do the same?"

"Can't."

"Why not?"

"What else would I be?" Reid said it angrily, but his eyes showed hurt and fear.

Jaxon framed Reid's face with his palms. "You'd be you. Reid Stanfill. That's more than enough."

Glowering, Reid pulled away slightly. "You're talking something serious when we've only known each other for a few days."

"We could spend a year doing dinner and a movie and long walks on the beach and I wouldn't get to see the real you as well as I have already. I guess being on the lam tends to strip away layers of pretense. We know each other better than anyone else on this planet knows us. And I like what I know." But since the discussion was moot anyway and he didn't want to argue, he kissed Reid's nose and got out of bed. "I need another shower."

Once they were clean and dressed and fed, the apartment held little to distract them. Shelves held a few books, but Jaxon couldn't read them and Reid said they were boring political tracts anyway—simplistic stories about the supposed achievements of Talmirov and his father. Reid and Jaxon tidied up the small messes they'd made, including gathering up the bedding for the laundry. Jaxon could have entertained them by singing, but he wanted to save his voice for that night. And for once, he wasn't at all in the mood to write new songs, probably because he knew he'd never perform them. They spent their time leafing through several photo albums full of strangers, wondering who the people were and what had become of them.

At midafternoon, Reid cooked a meal and badgered Jaxon to eat, but he wasn't hungry.

Between the apartment's small size and all the big furniture, there wasn't enough room to pace properly, and since the windows had to remain curtained, it precluded brooding while gazing through the glass. Out of desperation, Jaxon attempted to pick fights with Reid, who refused to take the bait.

By nightfall Jaxon was ready to claw his own skin off. But then someone knocked softly on the door and he desperately wished he had another few hours alone with Reid. Maybe Reid felt the same, because he cast Jaxon a long look before opening the door.

It was time to go.

THE apartment where they'd spent the night was several miles from the main square where Talmirov had decreed the concert would be held. Although now there was a slightly different agenda. Fedir and Lera accompanied them and confirmed that the word had gotten out—anyone who was interested in Jaxon Powers or in getting rid of Talmirov should assemble in the square. The tech guys were ready to do their thing, hijacked internet and all. Now the only problem was getting Jaxon and Reid to the square in a timely manner without being intercepted.

"We can't take the truck?" Jaxon asked as they descended the stairway.

"No," Fedir answered from two steps below. "Trucks are not normal in city center at night." He looked over his shoulder with a grin. "Tonight you go like real Vasnytsian."

It turned out that meant traveling by tram.

During the endless city tours, Jaxon had seen the trams creaking around on miles of tracks. They looked old, dirty, and tired, and they always seemed to be crammed with weary locals. They certainly wouldn't be ideal hiding spots, seeing as they had big windows, trundled slowly, and made lots of stops. But Lera was hot on the idea. "Nobody looks for Jaxon Powers in trams."

Reid shrugged. "Doesn't seem any riskier than anything else."

Jaxon made sure his jacket was zipped, and did his best to disguise himself. Since he'd lost his hat somewhere along the way, Fedir gave him a new one when they reached the bottom of the stairway. He also handed Jaxon a scarf, a welcome accessory against the evening chill.

The tram stop was only a block from the apartment, and several people already waited there, perhaps on their way to evening work shifts. None of them spoke, and they paid no attention to the newcomers—Lera and Fedir in coveralls, Jaxon and Reid in tracksuits, all of them trying to look mired in drudgery instead of like fugitives.

After about ten minutes, the tram rattled up. A few passengers got off and everyone at the stop climbed on. If anyone paid, Jaxon didn't see it. Either they all had passes or the citizens of Starograd were terrible fare evaders. Or maybe public transportation was free. As if that mattered to him now. All the seats were taken, so they held on to poles in the middle, Lera and Fedir doing their best to block Jaxon and Reid from view.

After starting with a lurch, the tram bumped and squeaked, stopping every few blocks. Even though the temperature was cool, the air inside felt too close, thick with the smells of cigarettes, sweat, and food. It made Jaxon long for the open spaces of the Sandhills, where the sky was enormous and the winds blew offensive odors away. He wished he could go there again and watch the grass rippling like a golden sea, with hawks soaring high above and storm clouds scudding in from the west. He used to love watching the lightning in the distance and feeling the hairs on his arms stand on end. Hearing the thunder as it simultaneously vibrated through his body as if he were a drum.

Once, when he was sixteen and a storm was on the way, he'd grabbed his guitar and driven his crappy old car out past the edge of town. Standing on a small bluff, he sang to the tempest until the rain and hail pelted him into submission. His mother yelled when he got home—"What on earth were you thinking? You could've been hit by lightning!"—and his father took the car keys for a month, but it had been worth it.

Another time he'd—

A ripple of unease ran through the tram, interrupting his reverie. He realized they'd stopped, but nobody was getting on or off. A gruff voice rang out at the far end of the car. Jaxon couldn't see what the fuss was, but Fedir was taller. Fedir hissed in English, "Go!"

Reid reacted while Jaxon was still trying to figure out what to do. Reid grabbed Jaxon's arm with one hand and pushed his way through the crowd with the other, dragging Jaxon with him. Nobody tried to stop them, and in fact a fuss at the other end of the car suggested that someone had impeded the shouter's progress. Reid and Jaxon hopped off the tram, Reid grunting on impact. They took off running, but after only a half block, Reid wheezed, "Can't keep up. Don't wait. Go!"

Somebody chased closely with pounding boots and barked orders. Jaxon gave Reid one last, desperate look and took off at top speed.

Other than music, running had always been the one thing Jaxon excelled at, and now he raced faster than ever before. He left his heart behind with Reid, who was slower under the best circumstances and still recovering from his injuries. Jaxon headed toward the bright lights that sprinkled the hill, hoping he'd reach the main square on the way.

Less than two blocks later, something whizzed past him, causing a small explosion in the plaster of a nearby wall. The sound took a moment to reach him, and only then did he realize someone was shooting at him. He swore, veered closer to the protection of the buildings, and ran faster than he would have thought possible.

More gunfire echoed behind him, followed by shouts and screams of pain. God, was that Reid? Jaxon couldn't tell through the rasp of his own breathing. He turned a sharp corner and for a split second considered going back to help. But what could he do? He was unarmed and completely unskilled in fighting, and he was no match for soldiers with guns. The best thing he could do was reach the main square and fulfill the mission. Anything else meant Reid was sacrificing himself for nothing.

Faster, dammit. Faster!

He left the noise of the fight behind.

Jaxon reached the old part of the city, where the streets were especially dark and narrow and alleys branched off at odd angles. This neighborhood was a rabbit warren. And Jaxon had to be faster than the foxes.

He zigged and zagged as much as possible while keeping a more or less direct route to the square. In the distance, sirens screeched with the piercing high-low keen he'd heard only in Europe. He didn't care. If he got to the square, he'd wail right back at them. He'd sing them all down with the truth.

Somewhere along the way, he lost his scarf and threw aside the hat. The chill wasn't bothering him now; he was sweating like at the end of a long, fast set. Barely slowing, he skimmed out of the jacket too. And he flew.

He became aware of a noise ahead of him—the unmistakable quiet rumble of a waiting crowd. Between his heated skin and straining lungs, he felt as if he were on fire. But he reached inside and found a final reserve of energy. He ran without feeling the pavement beneath his feet.

As he turned a corner, the street widened. Dozens of people standing shoulder to shoulder blocked his way, and he bounced ineffectually against the human barrier. He fell to his knees, then to all fours. He didn't even possess enough breath to cry.

People surrounded him. He couldn't make out their faces, couldn't understand any of their words. Then hands were lifting him to his feet, gentle but firm, and he caught two familiar words. "Jaxon Powers!" Repeated first by two or three people, then a dozen, then a hundred. Chanting in unison like a mantra or a prayer. Two men held Jaxon's arms to steady him, but it was the chanting that restored his energy and spurred him to walk. The crowd parted for him like the Red Sea for Moses, and walking to the beat of his own name, Jaxon headed into the square.

Chapter Sixteen

THE public space was more oblong than square, with an imposing stone building looming at one end. Jaxon suspected the building had originally been a church, but Talmirov disapproved of religion, so nowadays it housed dusty relics from Vasnytsia's past. Jaxon and Reid had toured it with Halyna, Jaxon more impressed by the architecture than the contents. But of course he wasn't going museum-hopping tonight. In front of the building was a stairway almost the width of the square itself, topped by a broad landing that made a natural stage.

Jaxon ascended the stairs under his own damn steam.

As he struggled to regain his breath, he looked around. The setup was primitive—a couple of big, battered speakers plugged into heavy-duty extension cords, a mic on a stand, a pair of spotlights, and a single acoustic guitar that looked brand-new. He'd had more sophisticated venues in junior high, but this would do.

The square was packed, and additional people stood at open windows and on balconies in the buildings around the square. A few even waved to him from rooftops. He waved back, and the crowd erupted in cheers.

Several streets converged at the square, and he saw red and blue lights flashing in some of them. Soldiers stood along the margins of the assembly, but none of the armed men were making any attempt to shut things down. Maybe because they didn't want to start a riot, or maybe because they were vastly outnumbered. In any case, they remained still and everyone ignored them.

After his desperate race, after losing Reid, Jaxon should have been capable of little more than curling into a ball and passing out. But he'd always drawn energy from his audiences, as though they were enormous batteries, and tonight was the biggest charge of all. These people hadn't plunked down money to hear a rock star sing a few favorite tunes. They'd come tonight risking their freedom, risking their *lives*, to listen to him. He wasn't going to let them down.

With a deep inhalation, Jaxon stepped forward and picked up the guitar. His audience cheered and clapped, the din reverberating off the adjacent buildings. He had to wait for the noise to fade before he could test the mic. "Zdravi Starograd!" he shouted, showing off his entire command of Vasnytsian with the simple greeting. But the crowd reacted as if he had performed a prodigious feat, everyone roaring approval. Again he had to wait for them to calm down before he could speak.

"I'm sorry I have to talk to you all in English. I hope you understand. And I want to thank all of you—the people of Vasnytsia—for your friendship. I know it's not easy for you to get access to my music, and it means so much to me that you make that effort. You are strong, kind people, and I'm so honored to have met you."

The ovation and cheering were so loud that Jaxon felt them throughout his body. Good. More energy.

He slung the guitar strap over his neck and spent a few minutes tuning the instrument. He'd played many of much higher quality, but this one felt good enough under his fingers. It would do just fine.

"I hope you don't mind, but I'm going to begin tonight with a brand-new song. I wrote it right here in Vasnytsia. It's called 'Battle Song,' and you're the first to hear me perform it." *And the last.* He forced a smile and began to strum the opening chords.

As always, he immediately lost himself in the song. The notes wove a magical spell and he was back in that castle, grieving the loss of his lover, waiting for the enemy soldiers to arrive. His throat wanted to tighten and keep the words inside, but he had the strength to overcome his tears. Still slightly winded from his run, with a crappy guitar and crappier sound system, he gave the best performance of his life—he felt it in his bones.

But as he neared the end of the final chorus, a strange thing happened, something that had never happened to him before. New words came as if carried by his muse, and he extemporized a new verse.

Even though the arrows take me,
Even though my songs are sung,
I carry love for a hero within me.

I bring you truth with my guitar and tongue.

The crowd applauded wildly. At least, Jaxon thought they did; he was too lost in his heart to be sure. And now, he knew, was the time for more direct words.

He searched near the base of the steps, and there in the corner nearest the building, hidden deeply in shadows, he spied a man and woman bent over a laptop. Jaxon descended the stairs. "Ready?" he asked.

The people with the laptop looked up at him. "I think so," the woman said.

"Do you want to give instructions?"

She hesitated, then squared her shoulders. "Yes." She walked up to the stage with him and the crowd hushed at once.

Speaking in front of a large assembly would terrify most people under any circumstances, even without armed men and antigovernment conspiracies thrown into the mix. But this woman took the mic and spoke in a clear, steady voice. Of course Jaxon couldn't understand most of it, but he caught his own name and the word *Wi-Fi*, and he saw the flurry of action as a large portion of the audience took out their cell phones and flipped them open. At the edges of the square, the soldiers shifted uneasily but didn't draw their weapons. Even the most trigger-happy among them must have been hesitant to fire into a large, nonviolent crowd. Jaxon wondered why the soldiers didn't just order the crowd to disperse, but perhaps they were afraid nobody would listen. Jaxon had the impression these people wouldn't scare easily.

But he also realized his time was limited, so as soon as the woman stepped away from the mic, Jaxon took over.

"I'd really rather sing to you than talk. I'm a better musician than I am a speaker. But I have to tell you these things. And God, I really hope the world is listening right now."

More movement from the soldiers, maybe more goal-directed now. Jaxon wouldn't have long to make his case, so he thought quickly, trying to be as succinct as possible.

"Your prime minister is corrupt. Talmirov has been stealing millions from you—from Vasnytsia. And he's been conspiring to help Russia invade sovereign nations." The crowd rumbled in response—anger, maybe, but not aimed at Jaxon. At the edges of the square, the soldiers became more forceful, trying to clear a path to him. The audience wasn't cooperating; in fact, it looked as if they were pushing back. But to Jaxon's left, closer to the stage, another commotion had begun. He couldn't make out what was going on there.

Doesn't matter, he reminded himself. *The message is the mission.*

He spoke louder. "My friend Reid has—" His voice broke over the verb tense, but he continued. "Reid has proof of what Talmirov's up to, but it's encoded and he can't get it out. They've tried to kill him over it. They might have already…." He couldn't say it.

Voices grew louder and angrier. Soldiers shouted at citizens, who shouted back. The jostling grew worse, like churning waves at the edges of a great dark sea. But nobody was trying to leave, and the vast majority of the audience held up their phones, waiting to broadcast what he said next.

"Vasnytsians are good people who don't deserve to live this way. World, don't turn your backs on them! This week a good man risked everything, has given up everything, just to show you the truth. Don't—"

The mic cut out with an earsplitting screech, and at the same time, the spotlights went dark. Now that the glare had gone, Jaxon could better make out what was happening in the square. Brightly lit windows in the surrounding buildings provided some illumination, as did hundreds of blinking and flashing lights from cell phone cameras. But what was happening in the square wasn't good. More uniformed men had arrived, and while they hadn't drawn their weapons, some of them were fortified with helmets and riot shields. Instead of trying to round up the bystanders, the soldiers seemed intent on getting to Jaxon.

Not much time left.

But dammit, the stage was still his, the audience still listening and still capturing him with their cameras. He had a robust voice; he could make it carry.

"Be strong!" he shouted. "Tyrants can't stand by themselves. There's so much life among you! So much good. And hope! I think the right side will never lose as long as there's hope. I—"

Several people near the stage called his name, distracting him. He turned to look and—Oh God. Reid was there, his T-shirt torn and bloodied, his face puffy and raw-looking. But he stood near the base of the stairs and waved his hand, and he was alive.

With the guitar still strapped around him, Jaxon rushed down the steps and into Reid's arms. Reid grunted at the impact and clutched him fiercely.

"You're not dead," Jaxon said.

"Not yet." Reid let go of him and looked around. "I need to get you out of here."

"No."

"Jax—"

"No point in running. I'm using my time wisely." He grabbed Reid's neck and yanked him close for a fierce kiss. "I love you."

Before Reid could argue, Jaxon raced back up the stairs. During the few moments he'd been offstage, more armed soldiers had arrived and come closer to the stage. But the crowd pressed tight around them, and now—Jaxon couldn't tell who started it—the people began to sing. It was "Dance One More for Me," the song he always used to close his gigs. Nothing could be more perfect.

Jaxon held up his hands and shouted, "Do what's right! Please help my friends!"

And then, because he had no words left to persuade his distant audience, he joined the present audience in song. His voice soared, enriched and supported by hundreds—thousands?—of others.

A weird little redheaded kid in rural Nebraska had once dreamed of being rich and famous, knowing deep in his heart that what he really longed for was love. But now he'd found something even better, something he hadn't dared hope for. Tonight Jaxon *mattered*, and that was the sweetest gift of all.

The chorus repeated again, the words as familiar to him as his own skin.

Don't leave me yet.

The guitars are still playing. The stars are still shining.

Dance one more.

Don't leave, don't leave me yet.

As he sang, Jaxon watched Reid, who had joined in the song as well.

The crowd began the song again and was midway through the first stanza when Jaxon was shot.

He didn't even realize it was a bullet at first. It felt like a blow to his shoulder, as if someone had punched him hard. He staggered back a few steps as everything slowed down, as the square went eerily silent. Then he felt the hot rush of blood and realized what had happened.

"Unusual way for a punk musician to die," he said quietly. He turned to look at Reid and smiled.

The second bullet knocked him to the ground.

The pain throbbed, yet distantly, like someone else's radio playing a block away. He felt as heavy as the stones of the castle as the crescent moon smiled down at him and... and....

Reid. Reid was there, tearing Jaxon's shirt open. Jaxon tried to reach for him, but his arm didn't seem to be working. "I broke the guitar," he said. It was in pieces, but parts of it were still attached to the strap behind his neck.

Reid worked the strap over Jaxon's head. "Hang on. Hang on, goddammit." His voice was so rough, but his hands were gentle as they moved over Jaxon's body.

Somewhere close by was a lot of shouting, a lot of frantic movement. Jaxon thought he caught his name, or maybe he just misheard some Vasnytsian. Didn't matter. "Did we do it? Did they hear us?"

"Yeah, Jax. They heard." Reid was doing something to Jaxon's wounds, but Jaxon couldn't tell what. His senses were all in a muddle. A cacophony of sound and sight and feeling—dull thuds of ache added to the sharper pain—and his mouth coppery with the taste of blood.

"Good," Jaxon mumbled.

"Don't leave me, babe. Don't."

Even though Reid's words were sad, Jaxon smiled at the sweetness of them, at the way they echoed his last song. He wondered when Reid had last used an endearment. He was going to ask—it seemed important for some reason—but suddenly men in uniforms loomed over Reid, who was too busy to notice.

"Reid," Jaxon croaked.

With a growl like an angry bear, Reid whirled around and flew at the nearest soldiers. But there were too many of them, and three quickly subdued him, shouting in Vasnytsian as he struggled.

"No," Jaxon cried weakly, trying without success to sit up. "Don't hurt him! He's—"

One of the soldiers fell to his knees beside Jaxon and pushed gently on his chest. "Do not move."

"You fuckers! Don't hurt Reid!" The effort made Jaxon gasp.

"No hurting," the soldier said. "We will help you." There was no cruelty in his eyes, just kindness and concern.

"Help?" said Jaxon, perplexed.

Then Reid called out to him. He'd stopped trying to fight the soldiers and now stood among them, unrestrained. "It's okay, Jax. They're on our side."

Jaxon's soldier grinned. "My wife is big fan of Jaxon Powers. She will kill me if I hurt you." Then his expression turned serious. "I know how bad Talmirov is. Many of us know."

"Oh." That was the best Jaxon could come up with. Thankfully, more conversation didn't seem expected.

"We must go now," the soldier said. "Not everyone is friend." Several of his colleagues came forward and lifted Jaxon into their arms. It hurt. And he was dizzy as they pushed their way quickly through the chaos. But the mission was complete, Jaxon had more friends than he'd realized, and Reid was right there, running alongside him.

Jaxon smiled.

Chapter Seventeen

"I DON'T think you translated that correctly." Jaxon shifted against the pillow and winced at the twinge of pain.

"Stop squirming," Reid said irritably. "You'll reopen the stitches. And my translation was accurate."

Dr. Kozel understood more English than she spoke. She nodded her agreement with Reid's statement.

"But… the guitar saved my life?"

"Probably." Reid frowned. "If that bullet had hit you straight on, it would have punctured your stomach and spleen. You'd have bled out right in the square. But it hit the guitar first, and that absorbed most of the impact."

"So all I got was a little dent."

"Not so little. But not fatal."

Jaxon used to think that music was his savior, but he'd never intended it so literally. "My shoulder hurts more than my torso."

"That's because you keep moving it. Stay still."

Reid left his bedside chair and crossed the room to Dr. Kozel. They talked softly, which wasn't necessary since they were speaking Vasnytsian. Jaxon sighed and tried again to get comfortable.

Four days had passed since the concert, and he was finally feeling good enough to be bored. The tiny hospital room offered little in the way of entertainment, with nothing but a few pieces of furniture, some beeping machines, and walls painted an ugly pale green. No television—not that he'd understand the programming anyway—and of course his cell phone was long gone. He didn't even have a window. For protection, Reid said. Maybe so, but Jaxon was ready to crawl out of his skin.

After several minutes of conversation, Dr. Kozel waved at Jaxon and left the room. Reid returned to his bedside, although he didn't sit down. He looked rough. Tired. He'd been pretty beat up in the altercation on the way to the main square, and he'd been sitting vigil with Jaxon ever since. But a bit of the tension had eased from his shoulders and jaw.

"The doc says you'll be okay to travel tomorrow. They'll have to dope you up a little, though."

"Hey, drugs. Isn't that what being a rock star is all about?"

Reid grunted. "I'd rather have you stay put a few more days, but things are unstable here. It's best if you get out ASAP."

"Best if *we* get out."

"The State Department's working on transport. We've been assured they'll let us cross the border, but... like I said, things are unstable. If all goes well, we'll have a nice short flight to Split."

"I like Croatia," Jaxon said. "Played a concert once in Zagreb. And I partied on a couple of the islands."

"No concerts this time, and definitely no partying."

"Yeah. It'll be a while before I can play anyway."

They'd performed surgery on his shoulder, and Dr. Kozel had assured him that with time and physical therapy, he'd recover well. But for now his left arm was mostly useless.

"You'll stay with me in Split?" It was more a demand than a question.

"Don't know," said Reid. "I'm going to need to spend a lot of time debriefing, and—"

"They can debrief you in Split. Or they can wait. I swear to God, if they try to drag you away from me, I will throw a celebrity tantrum of epic proportions." Jaxon paused. "Um, unless you don't want to be there."

"I do."

"Okay, then."

"But long-term, Jax, I can't—"

Jaxon stopped him with a raised right hand. "Forget long-term. I thought we'd both be dead days ago. I can take this one day at a time." That wasn't completely honest, but Jaxon was willing to postpone the issue. "Now, tell me what's up with our pal Talmirov."

REID didn't update him on Talmirov, not then. He tried several times to apologize for the shooting, until Jaxon was ready to take up arms himself just to make him stop. Instead he ended up guiding the conversation elsewhere by asking for details on what happened after they got off the tram. Reid tried to downplay his own actions, but the upshot was clear—he'd distracted two soldiers long enough for Jaxon to get a good lead, and when the distractions failed, he'd fought them. Both of them died from the blades he always seemed to be hiding somewhere.

When more *I'm sorry*s seemed imminent, Jaxon demanded details about the hospital. He was certainly grateful to the soldiers who rescued him, but he didn't understand how he'd received medical care without incident or arrest.

"One of the soldiers has family who works here," Reid explained. "And it turns out Talmirov's not popular among medical professionals. They get shitty pay, and he's refused them decent equipment and sufficient staff. We're lucky you pulled through."

And that was when Jaxon realized that not only was Reid blaming himself, he was exhausted. He might not have been shot, but he was pretty beat up and, unlike Jaxon, hadn't been given a chance to loll around in bed.

"Hey, Reid? Would you do me a favor?"

"Anything."

"Lie down next to me."

Reid rolled his eyes. "Jesus. You're in no shape to—"

"No touchy-feely or hanky-panky. I'm feeling a little overwhelmed and I need some comfort." It wasn't even a lie.

"I'm not a teddy bear," Reid grumbled, but he didn't hesitate to kick off his shoes. Taking great care not to move Jaxon too much, he settled onto the mattress. When Jaxon began humming a lullaby, Reid didn't even complain. He was asleep within minutes.

Jaxon dozed through the following morning, but as soon as he'd finished his bland lunch, a rush of activity began. People who were not hospital staff tromped in and out of his room and talked with Reid in Vasnytsian and a smattering of other languages. Jaxon knew they were discussing him, but he decided to stay in the background. It was like when he was on tour—he showed up whenever and wherever he was told.

Eventually a pair of orderlies lifted him onto a gurney.

"Can't I do a wheelchair? And real clothes?" he asked plaintively. Being wheeled out while flat on his back and wearing a hospital johnny wasn't his idea of a graceful exit.

"No unnecessary jostling," Reid answered firmly. But he didn't stop Jaxon from pausing to sign autographs or pose for selfies with members of the hospital staff, gurney and all.

Leaving the hospital required a roundabout path through various hallways before reaching a side door. An ambulance waited, and the orderlies quickly bundled Jaxon into the back. It appeared as if Dr. Kozel wanted Reid to ride up front, but he flat-out refused and got in the back with Jaxon.

The ride to the airport was short but bumpy. Jaxon wished they'd given him better drugs.

He was soon being wheeled toward a jet. But before he figured out how he was going to get inside, several figures came running across the tarmac. At first Reid tensed, but he relaxed as they came closer.

"Halyna!" Jaxon exclaimed when he recognized one of them.

She wore jeans and a lightweight sweater, not one of the uniform-like suits he'd seen her in before, and she was smiling. "I hoped I would get here before you left."

Jaxon had no idea what side anyone was on—or even what the sides were, exactly—but Halyna had been nice to him and didn't appear to be a threat now. The people accompanying her were gaping like fans, not getting ready to shoot him. They were in street clothes too.

"Are you all right?" he asked her.

"Yes, I think so. This is exciting time for my country, yes?"

"Yeah. But I think I've had enough excitement to last me awhile."

Her expression turned serious. "Thank you. For everything." She gave him a careful hug and kissed both his cheeks. Then she did the same for Reid.

The plane was nothing like the one that had brought them to Vasnytsia. In fact, it appeared to be a cargo plane, or maybe a military transport—Jaxon didn't get a good enough look at the outside to tell. The entry ramp was much easier for him than stairs would have been, and soon he was secured in the no-frills hold with Dr. Kozel and Reid in seats nearby.

"Less than an hour," Reid said, patting Jaxon's good shoulder.

As soon as they were in the air, Dr. Kozel fixed her gaze outside a window. Jaxon wondered how long it had been since she'd left the country—if ever. He was glad his injuries had given her the opportunity. She seemed swept up in the adventure.

True to form, however, Reid was uptight. He rearranged Jaxon's pillow several times, tucked and untucked the blankets, and kept asking him if he was okay.

Finally Jaxon grabbed his wrist. "Tell me what's going on in Vasnytsia. Politically, I mean."

Reid sighed and settled back in his seat. "Chaos, mostly. The videos from the main square went viral instantly. Thousands and thousands of hits within minutes. News agencies scrambled. It was still daytime back in the States—still working hours—and members of Congress popped up all over to speak out against Talmirov. It was a big deal, Jax. People across the world hanging on to their seats, waiting to hear if you were alive."

"Yeah, but what about Talmirov?"

"That night, people marched in the streets of Starograd. In some of the other cities too. And the military didn't do much about it. I think they weren't getting clear orders, and anyway, they didn't want to cause bloodshed. The marchers were their friends and relatives. Plus Talmirov didn't exactly inspire loyalty among the troops."

Jaxon sighed in relief. "So nobody else died."

"No. But by morning the prime minister's palace was under siege from protestors, and so were most of the government buildings. Talmirov gave a speech on TV denying everything, but nobody believed a word, and most of Europe was already denouncing him." He chuckled. "Russia issued a statement that denied any scheming."

It was kind of a shame Jaxon had missed all of that. He would have liked watching his new friends have their moment in the streets. "So then?"

"By the second night, all attempts at government control of the people had ended. People were playing music everywhere—folk songs, your songs, everything—and dancing. They're calling it the Dancing Revolution because it started with your song, sort of."

Shit. "Revolution?"

"Talmirov was gone by the next day, along with a bunch of his cronies. Now everyone's trying to figure out what to do next, but reasonable voices are prevailing.

They've already freed some dissidents from prison, and those men and women seem to be organizing things. I think it'll turn out okay." Reid nodded to emphasize his point.

It wasn't the good drugs making Jaxon feel warm and fuzzy now—it was the knowledge that he'd helped bring about something good. Fedir and Lera, Halyna, even that ever-scowling barista from the Black Cat, they wouldn't have to hide out in basements any longer.

But that raised a less pleasant thought. "Albina's dead. And Mariya—"

"Mariya is fine. She was in a holding cell when the shit hit the fan, but she hadn't been harmed. She was one of the people freed. She's in hiding now, and I don't know where, but she managed to get word to me that she's safe."

Jaxon let out a long sigh of relief. "Does anyone know where Talmirov went?"

"Russia, probably, although they won't admit it. Other governments are going to put a lot of pressure on Moscow to hand him over for trial. And once that damn chip is out of my arm, the proof will be out there. Moscow's going to have a lot of incentive to play nice."

If Reid sounded a little smug, Jaxon couldn't blame him. In fact, picturing Talmirov in prisoner orange was damned satisfying.

Jaxon must have spaced out on that image for a time, because before he knew it, the plane was bumping to a landing.

The confusing scene on the tarmac involved Croatian police of some kind, Croatian medical personnel, and Croatian and American officials. Reid stuck close to Jaxon and refused to allow anyone to badger him.

After another brief ambulance ride, Jaxon rejoiced to discover that instead of a dreary hospital, his destination was a lovely villa with a view of the sea. Although medical equipment flanked Jaxon's bed, the room also boasted large windows overlooking a pool and garden. There was a flat-screen TV. And, one of the Americans showed him with pride, a new smartphone to replace the one he'd lost in Starograd.

"It's like I won the showcase on a game show. Where's my brand-new car?"

The Croatians seemed confused, but Reid snickered at the joke.

Eventually Jaxon settled in his temporary new home and the officials cleared out, leaving him alone with Reid, except for housekeeping staff and some nurses. Dr. Kozel pronounced the new arrangements satisfactory, and Jaxon thanked her. She left, presumably to enjoy a nice little seaside vacation.

"I'm wiped," Jaxon said. "I'm usually cool with travel, but—"

"But you're not usually shot full of holes."

"I'm not *full* of holes. That's an exaggeration." Jaxon yawned hugely. "But it's still tiring, apparently. Shit. It's not even dinnertime. Hey, do you think we can get squid ink risotto here? I love that stuff."

Reid shook his head. "Rest. A lot of people are eager to talk to you."

Yeah. Among other things, Jaxon figured he and Buzz needed to have a long conversation. "Fine." He patted the other side of the bed. "Join me."

"I have to get the chip out. And then debriefing, and—"

"Yeah, yeah. But come join me."

Reid gazed out the window as if he were fascinated with the landscaping. Somewhere along the line he'd gotten his hands on jeans and a white button-down. The look flattered him, but then what didn't?

"We talked about this, Jax." Still facing away. "We can't do this. Our lives are on different tracks."

"I can change my track. I wasn't all that satisfied with where my train was going anyway."

"I can't ask you to give up being… Jaxon Powers."

"I'm always gonna be him. I could move back to Peril, work in my dad's insurance office, maybe farm some acreage, and I'd still be Jaxon Powers. With an x."

Reid finally turned around. "And your music?"

"I've proved I can be a superstar. Look, I could do a weekly gig for friends in Terry Holcomb's barn and be just as happy as in an arena somewhere."

Rubbing his chin—his stubble was becoming a beard—Reid crossed the room and sat beside him. "You're not what I expected. I thought you were a spoiled, rich brat. I thought you didn't care about anything but getting high and throwing money around. And fucking anyone who came near."

"Yeah?" The words didn't hurt. A lot of people probably thought the same. Hell, to some extent that had been him, once upon a time.

"That's not you at all. You're brave. Stupid about it sometimes, but brave. You care about people, and I don't mean the kind of people who get awards and show up in gossip columns. Regular people. And your music…. You're not some lucky poser who's been groomed to meet marketing algorithms. When you sing you're offering your soul, naked for the world to see." He sighed. "It's beautiful."

"Then why is this a problem?" Jaxon asked softly.

"Because I'm not the man you deserve." His eyes filled with tears that didn't overflow.

Jaxon's throat felt tight and his next words came out choked. "You're more than I deserve. And you're exactly what I want. More. You're what I need."

After a pause, Reid stroked a curl away from Jaxon's forehead. Such a tender touch from a hand that had been trained to be so strong. "I'm finding myself wondering how I lived all these years without you," he said. "But I need some time. Not to decide how I feel about you—I know that part. I need to decide how I feel about myself."

Jaxon grasped that hand with his own and brought it to his lips for a soft kiss on the knuckles. "I can give you time. I'm not going anywhere. Whenever you're ready, we'll catch that metaphorical train together."

Instead of replying, Reid returned the kiss, this time a tender brush against Jaxon's knuckles. Then he let go, stood, and crossed to the door. After one long look over his shoulder, he was gone.

Chapter Eighteen

WAKING up in a Croatian villa should have been wonderful. The air smelled of lavender and the sea, Jaxon's breakfast was a variety of fresh fruit, and the nurse, who was a handsome man with dimples, helped him walk to the bathroom instead of making him use a bedpan. The sun shone brightly in a sharp blue sky. Jaxon's iPhone was close at hand, ready to connect him to the world. The setting was infinitely nicer than anywhere he'd slept for the past number of days—forests, ruined castles, basements, oppressive hotels, rabbit-hutch apartments, and boring hospitals.

But Reid wasn't here.

Oh, he was alive and well, which was enormously comforting. But he wasn't in Jaxon's room. That hurt worse than getting shot, even though Jaxon held out hope he'd return soon.

Still, Jaxon tried to behave himself. He spoke at length with some friendly people from the State Department. Although he had some negative opinions to share about their colleague Diana Chiu, who'd dragged him into this mess with half-truths and lies, he couldn't really blame her or any of them. The mission, right?

He ate a lovely lunch of grilled fresh sardines. Then he argued with one of his nurses, who didn't want to open the windows in case Jaxon got a chill.

"It's warm enough and I want fresh air. If you don't open them, I will."

The nurse made a face, but she opened the windows. With a breeze ruffling the curtains and playing over his skin, Jaxon took a short nap.

After he woke up and had a bandage change and sponge bath, a woman from the US Embassy came to his room. "Are you feeling well?" she asked in a Croatian accent. She was a grandmotherly sort, short and plump and cardiganed.

"I am. Everybody here's treating me amazingly well."

"We are happy to have you as a guest. We've obtained a new passport for you, so you'll be able to leave when you're ready. But no hurry. Enjoy Dalmatia while you recover."

"I will," he said with a smile. "Can't think of a better place to recuperate."

"Excellent. I have a… special visitor for you. If you feel up to it."

"Sure."

She stepped out, and Jaxon expected her to return with a Croatian bigwig of some kind, or maybe the US ambassador. Instead, a thin woman with gray hair entered hesitantly. She wore slacks and a pale blue blouse and held her large purse in front of her like a shield.

Jaxon's mouth went dry. "Mom?" he croaked.

He hadn't seen her in twenty years, but neither her short hairstyle nor the oversize glasses had changed much. When she came closer, he caught a whiff of Shalimar, which he remembered his father buying for her birthday every year.

"Jaxon." Her voice shook. "Is it all right that I'm here?"

"Yes. God, yes, Mom."

That set them both to crying. He'd never seen her cry before. And they hugged, which hurt his wounds but was a balm to his soul, and then she sat beside him.

"Your father couldn't come but he sends his love." She dabbed her eyes with a tissue. "He does."

"Tell him I love him too."

"I will. His health has been poor lately, or he would have come."

Time to mourn lost years later. Jaxon gave a small smile. "Maybe I can come visit after I'm healed. If you want me to."

"We do."

She reached for his hand and he gave it to her. At one time he'd been so angry at them, but he'd come to realize that their experiences and circumstances imprisoned them. Perhaps, if Jaxon had been patient, they might have opened the doors to that prison, but he had fled as soon as he was able.

"Thanks for coming here, Mom. It's a long way from Peril."

"We saw you on the television. Nobody knew then if you were even alive, and...." She sniffled into the tissue. "And your father and I were devastated.

You never think your child will go before you do. You always assume you'll have a chance to mend fences."

"We can mend them now. But it has to be two-way. It's taken me a long time, but I'm comfortable with who I am. I won't try to change that." He was proud that his voice didn't waver even though his emotions ran wild.

Still clutching his hand, she nodded. "I think your father and I would very much enjoy getting to know you. We've been told you're a remarkable man."

They spoke for another hour, catching up on family gossip. His father had some heart and back problems, which was why he couldn't travel, and Jaxon was relieved the news wasn't worse. As they talked, an empty place deep inside Jaxon began to fill, a small starvation now fed.

But he was still weak, the emotions were overwhelming, and his mother caught him yawning. "You shouldn't overdo it. I'll let you rest." She let go of his hand and stood.

"Will you come back after I'm rested?"

"Of course." She smiled widely. "I might be a tourist in the meantime. Who'd have thought someday I'd be in Croatia!"

"Enjoy, Mom. Come back for dinner?"

"I'd love to."

"Good. What are your thoughts on squid ink?"

AFTER another nap, Jaxon became restless. He persuaded his nurse to help him walk a few circuits of the room, but that was as much as his body could take. And his mind… his mind didn't know what to do. Rejoice over being alive? Celebrate Vasnytsia's freedom? Brood over Reid? Delight in reconciling with his parents? It was all too much, like being immersed in a whirlpool and trying to snatch at one particular fish.

However, he could accomplish a few things even now.

Jaxon picked up his new phone and punched in a number he'd memorized long ago. It rang only once.

"Jaxon! My darling! Oh my *God*, how are you doing?"

"I'm doing okay, Buzz."

"I wanted to come see you, but they're being very top-secret about where you are, and I couldn't even reach you because your number went straight to voicemail, and oh my God, I've been so worried, I'm going to find that Chiu woman and kick her a new asshole because how dare she do this to you and—"

"Breathe, Buzz. I said I'm okay."

Buzz tsked. "I saw you gunned down, baby boy."

"I got back up again."

For a while Buzz gushed a lot of words. Hearing him made Jaxon smile. Yes, Buzz could be melodramatic and a bit over the top, but he cared about Jaxon and had always done right by him, an achievement not always shared by others in the business.

Finally even Buzz had to take a break, so Jaxon hurried to get his own words in. "Hey, can you do something for me?"

"Anything, cupcake. I'll get you anything you need."

"When things settle down in Vasnytsia and everything's safe, will you arrange a concert for me there? Maybe more than one, I don't know. Free and open to the public."

Buzz paused briefly before responding with skepticism in his voice. "I wouldn't think you'd ever want to step foot in that place again."

"No, see, I like the place. And the people. And… they had a lot of faith in me, you know? Risked everything for me. I want to pay some of that back."

Buzz paused a moment before answering in a tone more somber than usual. "You got it, honey. As soon as we can pull it off without you getting shot at, you're there."

"Thanks." Maybe Jaxon should learn some of the language before then. He wouldn't have Reid to interpret.

He leaned a little deeper into his pillows, twitching his shoulder to find a comfortable angle. And he closed his eyes as he thought about filling some of the other holes in his psyche.

"Another thing, Buzz. When I'm back in the States, I'd like to look for a place to buy. A home. Can you help me with that?"

"Of course. Where were you thinking? What kind of place?"

"I don't know." A castle on a hill, with his lover to sing to sleep at night.

"I'd kind of like a mountain cabin," a familiar voice said.

Jaxon's eyes flew open and he gaped at the man who'd crept to his bedside. Reid stood there in a suit, a bouquet of lavender clutched in his hand, a hesitant smile on his lips. Wrinkles marred his dress shirt, his slacks had lost their careful pleat, and another day's worth of beard scruff darkened his face. God, he was beautiful.

Nobody said anything at all for a long moment. But then Buzz called his name. "Jaxon? Jaxon! Is something wrong?"

Surprisingly, Jaxon found his voice. "I think something's right. I hope."

Reid nodded.

"You sound strange, kid. What's going on?"

"I'm… I'm gonna have to get back to you. I'll call you soon." Jaxon ended the call and set the phone aside. "Mountain cabin?" he said after a moment. His throat rasped as if he'd just completed a concert. He wanted to reach out to Reid but didn't quite dare, as if Reid was a fever-dream that might disappear.

"Yes. A chalet with balconies and a huge fireplace, and acres of trees all around. Owls hooting at night." Reid ducked his head, then raised it again. "Or a high-rise condo. Or a bungalow by the beach. A suburban split-level. A farmhouse in Nebraska. I don't really care all that much, actually. Long as you're there."

Strange. Jaxon felt shockier now than when he'd been bleeding onto the pavement. Good thing he wasn't hooked up to a heart monitor anymore. "No more different tracks?"

"Changed my ticket. Open itinerary. I go wherever you go."

"That's a fast switch. You've figured yourself out already?"

"I figured enough."

"How?"

Reid set the flowers on the bedside table and knelt beside him. He worked the fingers of one hand into Jaxon's curls, and God, just that small contact was almost enough make Jaxon cry. "Pivo," said Reid.

"What?"

"Pivo. It means beer. I left here yesterday because I thought I was doing the right thing. But every damn time I closed my eyes, even just to blink, I saw you being shot. I remembered when I thought I'd lost you." He snorted. "So I drank a whole lot of pivo last night. Enough that it should have washed that vision away. But it didn't. I could drink an entire ocean of the stuff and I'd still... I'd still feel you."

"I feel you too."

"I know. But this morning I was walking along the Riva—along the waterfront, in front of Diocletian's palace."

Jaxon touched Reid's arm. "I know the place."

"Diocletian gave up being emperor of Rome, you know? Chose to retire here instead."

"In luxury."

"Yes. I wonder if it made him happy? Anyway, I'm still not sure I'm the right man for you. Don't know that I'm… enough."

"More than." Dammit, now Jaxon *was* starting to cry. Second time today. He hadn't cried when he'd been *shot*, for fuck's sake.

"Yes, well, I can work at it. I'm pretty good at fulfilling a mission once I've set my mind to it. Because the thing is, you're the right man for me. Being with you doesn't weaken me—you make me strong. You're… this thing that's missing from me. You're it." His eyes were wet too. He rubbed impatiently at them with the back of his free hand.

Scratchy-voiced, Jaxon asked, "So what do we do?"

"We get to know each better, without anyone trying to kill us while we're at it."

"We go out on dates? Dinner and a movie?" Jaxon was only half joking, because it turned out that the boy from Nebraska secretly yearned for a dose of old-fashioned normalcy.

"Dinner and a movie. You'll impress me with tales about all the famous people you know, and then I'll impress you with my spy stories."

Jaxon could picture it—the two of them eating a good meal, laughing as they talked, both of them knowing that as soon as they got home they'd fall into bed together. It was a beautiful picture. "What else?"

Reid spread his arms wide. "Everything else. The whole world, Jax. We go wherever we want. Or we stay put if we'd rather. We buy that house you were just talking about. We build our future. We find our way together."

"Together." Jax breathed it like a sacred word.

"Yeah."

"I like that mission. I like it a lot."

They kissed tenderly. Reid's lips were still bruised and Jaxon could only embrace him with one arm. Didn't matter. Best kiss ever.

Then Reid climbed in beside him and they snuggled. They could save their words and plans for later. The specifics of the mission could wait. They had as long as they wanted.

As Jaxon lay there, listening to Reid's steady breaths and strong heartbeat, a tune formed in his head, followed by words. Words about love and hope and dreams, about building a home together. They were kind of sappy, actually, but that was just fine for an intimate concert.

Maybe Reid would add some verses of his own.

Coming in November 2018

Dreamspun Desires #69
Seeking Solace by Ari McKay

All hands on deck for a shipboard romance—with a secret.

Like his cousins, Devin Walker aspires to be a chef, but he wants to indulge his wanderlust while feeding his customers, and working a cruise ship seems like the solution. Since he can't find an opening in the kitchen, he's happy to start out in a position behind the bar.

While onboard *Poseidon's Pearl*, Devin is assigned to shepherd a visiting executive. Paul Bailey is quiet and unassuming, and a car accident that cost him his leg also shattered his confidence. He doesn't think he's attractive to other men anymore, and Devin is eager to show him just how wrong he is. But Paul has a surprising secret, and it might sink their passionate affair before it even makes it out of port.

Dreamspun Desires #70
Femme Faux Fatale by Susan Laine

Mystery. Murder. Men in silk stockings. Hollywood nights are heating up.

Hardboiled Los Angeles PI Cain Noble is hired by wealthy and gorgeous Camille Astor to find her husband and a priceless work of art—both of which have disappeared.

At the nightclub owned by Mr. Astor, Cain encounters the mesmerizing Lily Lavender, who has the body of a goddess and the sultry voice of an angel—but is really a young man named Riley who attracts trouble like a magnet.

What's a private dick in the vein of LA's bygone era and a cross-dressing burlesque starlet to do when faced with the hidden decadence and lethal dangers of the Hollywood Hills? They have their work cut out because they haven't even scratched the surface of an elaborate scheme more twisted than anyone could ever have imagined.

Love Always Finds a Way

◉REAMSPUN DESIRES
Subscription Service

Love eBooks?

Our monthly subscription service gives you two eBooks per month for one low price. Each month's titles will be automatically delivered to your Dreamspinner Bookshelf on their release dates.

Prefer print?

Receive two paperbacks per month! Both books ship on the 1st of the month, giving you *exclusive* early access! As a bonus, you'll receive both eBooks on their release dates!

Visit
www.dreamspinnerpress.com
for more info or to sign up now!